THE HANGING TREE

BY

MAUREEN
PIERCE STUVEL

Editing by *Exact Edits*. Lindsey Nelson

Book Cover Design by ebooklaunch.com

ISBN 978-1-7341574-0-6

Dedication

To my amazing husband, Kevin,
and our three wonderful children
Chelsea, Michael, and Travis,
whose love and support
helped me accomplish my dream.

Special appreciation to my friends
Tom, Mary, Melinda, Donna, Renee, and Janice
for all their support and encouragement.

CHAPTER 1

THE BEGINNING AND THE END

I laid my cheek against the chilly ceramic tile of the hospital room; a cloud seemed to loom around me. All I could hear were the faint beeps of the heart monitor hooked to my husband and the pumping of his ventilator. I wanted to go to his bedside, but I couldn't.

The day kept flashing before me like a constant rerun. I continued to question myself: *Could I have stopped this from happening? Had I told him what I'd seen, would he have stayed home, maybe taken a different route to work, or just laughed me off as he strolled out the door?* The guilt, along with the stark reality, made me sick to my stomach.

My thoughts were screaming at me: *Why? Why him? Why didn't I say something? Why am I cursed with this so-called ability?*

If that's what it really is, *ability...*

Since I was young, I've had flashes of scenarios moments before they happened, or dreams of situations, people, and major events that I would see again days or weeks later when they became reality. By merely touching the forearm or elbow of someone I've just met, I'm able to see their mental well-being. It's as if I can see the holes in their souls beneath their skin, even through the smiles they paste on their faces. The hardest thing to cope with is when people act as if they're my friends to my face, although I know they're not being genuine, which is not really so unusual I guess—many people have that insight. But my intuition led me to see *how* they would betray me, before it actually happened. Still, in most cases, I would continue with the relationship because I wanted to be wrong.

Whatever I was seeing or feeling or picking up through my alien antenna, I hated it all! People told me I had a gift. Even though I never shared my so-called talent or gift with anyone in casual conversation, after a certain age, I knew it was weird and wanted nothing to do with whatever was going on in my mind. Besides, it wasn't like I was picking up things 24/7, so maybe it was all a fluke. It could just be a lucky guess. People called me insightful and kind, but I still didn't have very many friends, so I figured I couldn't be all that great. People would call me and unload all their personal dilemmas on me as if I were "Dear Abby" or a personal shrink. They'd do this as they were driving to a friend's house or a party or somewhere else they would never think to ask if I wanted to be invited to. I never turned down helping them though, but I did start to feel resentful, thinking this gift would always keep me from making true friends. I just wanted to be normal, whatever that was…

Then I met my husband, Joel; I was twenty-two, and he was twenty-eight. We became friends, and then it moved to lovers, then life companions. He was kind and generous and everything I was looking for in a man. I told him about things that happened in the past that I'd known would occur before they actually did. I just wanted to test the waters to see how he would react. I could tell he was skeptical and didn't believe in people being able to tell the future, but he listened. After witnessing a few of these odd experiences, he had more respect for me, but there was never actual acceptance about this "gift," so I kept quiet about it. In fact, for years, I tried to stifle any recognition I'd have with people or events and brushed it all off as just coincidence. But under the surface, it was always there, waiting to break through and be discovered.

As time went on, I started to realize—or maybe I just grew up—that this wasn't the curse I had always made it out to be. It was a gift—I believe a gift from God. I started to view it as a path to help people. I was never a religious sort. I was raised Catholic; I believed in God but never ran around spewing Bible passages. However, with age comes an aspect of spirituality; you realize your own mortality and that there's a lot you don't know. I started to open myself up to that fact.

I wasn't ready to jump in headfirst and declare myself a supernatural being. I still wasn't comfortable with whatever you wanted to call what I had: *ability...gift...*or what I came to feel most comfortable with—a *calling*. I know that sounds like I'm entering the priesthood, but it truly felt like a calling. When I hear, see, or dream about something or someone, it's like they're asking for help or giving me a warning or knowledge to pass on. It wasn't like I could read people's minds; it's more feelings, signals. When it came down to it, I wasn't sure what exactly it was. I hadn't spent time trying to develop or hone the skill; I just wanted to help people.

The hospital door pushed open, waking me from my daydream. I popped my head off the wall. There stood the thin, pale-faced blue-eyed nurse who'd been so kind.

"Are you okay?" she asked.

I nodded my head.

She glanced over to where my husband lay in bed. I could tell she thought it strange that I had positioned myself across the room from him, especially since they'd brought in a comfortable chair so I could sit at Joel's side. She was polite and never asked why I was so far away from him.

"Have your kids arrived?" she asked.

"No, they should be here soon," I said. Although, I truly had no concept of time and how long ago I had called them or even what time of day it was. I just knew I didn't feel like talking and was trying to give the shortest answer with the least amount of explanation necessary.

"Would you like me to stay with you?" She smiled, reaching over and grasping my hand with a gentle, compassionate squeeze.

As she clutched my hand, I could feel the sincerity of her heart and the genuine empathy she felt for my situation. I looked at her, thinking that I couldn't even remember her name, and yet I felt closer to her right then than some people I've known my whole life. I glanced down at her nametag and saw *Jena* engraved in white.

"Thank you, Jena. You've been wonderful, but I would really just like to be alone for a little longer," I said.

"Would you like me to bring you a pillow? You could sit in the chair and put it behind your head," Jena asked. It was her way of trying to gently coax me to my husband's side.

"No," I said in a soft voice. "I'll be fine; I'll sit down in a moment." This seemed to appease her, as she again gently squeezed my hand and left the room.

As she walked out, I felt a little guilty for not learning her name during the night. She was so wonderful and accommodating. With her long coal-black hair rimming her pale face, she almost reminded me of the Goth kids I taught, except without the black makeup and long leather trench coats. I paused for a moment, wondering if she was a past student. I'd been teaching high school for years, and it was so incredible to see my past students as adults, living adult lives. I always felt like I never changed, but my students changed so much. I would think she would've said something if she were a former student. As those thoughts faded, the reality of my husband's impending death hung heavy in the room.

I moved to the foot of his bed. As I looked at him, with all the tubes and machines running in and out of his body, I thought, *Could I have changed all this?* Two nights ago, I'd had a horrible nightmare—Joel was in an awful car accident. Everything was so real and vivid, as if I were standing on the street corner witnessing the whole thing as it unfolded.

I watched as the firemen cut him from the wreckage of his car. The EMTs loaded him into the back of the ambulance, one saying, "I don't know about this one. Maybe we should have called in flight for life."

"We'll have the hospital make that call; let's just get him there," his partner replied.

As they drove away, I looked up at the street signs: 17th Avenue and Main Street. My husband turned left there every day on his way to work.

I'd woken up in a sweat. I'd had several very vivid random dreams like that in the past; not all came true, but it was certainly enough to give me pause. Most of the time, my dreams were bits and pieces of things, and I had to put them together like a puzzle. This dream, however, seemed like I had stepped out of my body and was actually part of the scene.

That morning, I had taken a day off from school to get caught up on my grading, so I'd tried to talk Joel into playing hooky from work.

"I can't. I have some engineers coming in from Korea, and I'm going to meet with them all day," Joel had said.

"Okay. What if we just go out for breakfast, and you go in late?"

I thought if I altered the dream, there was no way it would happen. So, if I were with him, he would be safe.

"No, honey, I'm sorry. I'm not going to be your excuse for you not getting caught up on your grading," he said with a smile and a chuckle.

"It's not that...I just have one of those feelings."

He knew what I meant. He paused and looked at me. I knew it gave him a little cause for thought. He stared at the floor, searching for his reply. Then he gave me a kiss on the forehead, looked into my eyes, and said, "I'll be just fine. Don't worry."

I grabbed his forearm and pulled him toward me. In that instant, I saw his face at the moment of impact during the accident. The fear of what was happening permanently imprinted in his features.

"Please don't go," I said. "We could have some great fun today." I pushed my mouth to his in a long kiss.

He laughed and said, "Don't get me started."

I was being coy. Why hadn't I just come right out and told him about the dream? I cannot believe, after all these years, I'm still afraid of judgment, not wanting him to think he married a fruit loop.

Joel smiled and walked toward the door; my son John popped out of his room, announced he was late for school, gave me and his father a kiss on the cheek, and an *I love you both* as he dashed to his car.

Joel turned and chuckled to himself. He told me he loved me and not to worry so much.

"Oh, and by the way, get your homework done," he said with a grin.

"Very funny," I responded.

I walked to the window and watched him drive away. Thinking it was just a dream, I let it go.

At nine o'clock, the phone rang; my knees buckled as I tried to get up and answer it.

I knew...

I just knew...without talking to anyone. I knew...

The voice on the other end of the phone was that of a young state-patrol officer.

"Hello, is this Mrs. O'Reilly?"

"Yes, I'm Sara O'Reilly." My voice was already shaking.

"This is Officer Doug Jones from the Colorado State Patrol, and I need to inquire if you are related to Joel O'Reilly."

"Yes, he's my husband." Tears started to stream down my face. "Is he alive?" I blurted out.

"Yes, ma'am, he's alive. However, he was involved in a very serious car accident at the corner of 17th and Main this morning."

I fell to my knees, and, almost doubling over from the instant pain in my stomach, I dropped the phone.

I could hear the officer on the phone calling out, "Mrs. O'Reilly? Mrs. O'Reilly, are you okay?"

I picked up the phone from the floor. He was asking if I would be okay to drive myself. "Yes," I replied and then asked about Joel's injuries. He said it would be best if I talked to hospital personnel about that.

I hung up the phone and grabbed my purse and cell phone. I called my oldest daughter, Ann, who's a high school English teacher; her cell was off. *What am I thinking? She's in class; of course, it's off.* I didn't want to deliver that kind of message via voicemail, so I hung up and called my son David.

David was in college, and I knew he didn't have any morning classes, but he was fifty miles away. What would I say? I knew I needed to stay calm because I didn't want him driving like a madman to the hospital.

David picked up on the fourth ring. "Hello," he said sleepily.

"David," I said in the calmest voice I could muster.

"Mom, what's up?"

I took a deep breath. "David, your father's been in an accident."

"What? Is he okay? How did it happen?"

I had no answers for those questions yet.

"I know very little right now. I'm on my way to the hospital. I need you to do a few things for me."

"Anything, Mom," he replied.

"Go to your sister's school, and tell her what happened. Then go to your brother's school, and get him; all three of you should be at the hospital. In the meantime, I'll try to get as much information as possible and relay it to you."

"Mom?"

"Yes, David."

"Is Dad going to be okay?"

"I'm sure everything will be fine. Just drive carefully and meet me at the hospital."

I knew I had a couple of hours before the kids would get to the hospital. This would give me time to find out how bad things were and to get myself together before they arrived.

When I arrived at the hospital and asked about my husband's condition, I was met with a barrage of paper work.

"I just want to see my husband, and yes, we do have insurance! I'll fill this crap out later!" I shouted.

A doctor appeared then and was very apologetic. "Are you Joel O'Reilly's wife?"

"Yes I am."

"I'm sorry about all this, Mrs. O'Reilly. The receptionist is new, and they impress upon them so much that every *I* has to be dotted and every *T* crossed."

"Please, just tell me about my husband!"

"I'm sorry to tell you that your husband has a considerable closed-head injury, among other injuries."

"What are the other injuries?"

"He has a collapsed left lung, a broken left femur, a severe puncture wound to his left side, and possible broken pelvis. He has severe swelling and bleeding in his brain, which is our main concern at this point. Mrs. O'Reilly, we need to operate to try to control the bleeding and swelling," the doctor said, looking directly in my eyes.

"What are his chances?" I asked.

He took a long, slow breath. "I'm not going to sugarcoat things; that's just not the kind of doctor I am. Your husband has suffered an extreme amount of trauma; I'm going in to try to save his life. However, his chances of survival are low but not nonexistent. I tell people in this situation to pray for the best, but prepare for the worst."

It felt as though he'd just stabbed me, but I appreciated his honesty. One warm tear streamed down my face. It was as if my whole body was in such shock that it couldn't give more than one tear.

The doctor asked if I wanted to see him before surgery. I nodded my head; words were difficult. He led me through some automated doors and down a corridor of rooms. The hallway seemed like a cavern, but it appeared to narrow as we proceeded. I turned into the room, and there lay Joel on a bed surrounded by machines and nurses. The nurses paused and looked at me as I entered, their faces painting the mood of the situation. I grabbed Joel's hand, which had an IV inserted, and just for a moment, I looked at it. The hand where I had placed a wedding ring twenty-five years ago, a ring that never came off his hand.

"Where's his ring?" I asked.

"We put it with his belongings," the nurse said.

My eyes slowly went from his hand up his arm, where I saw a splattering of dried blood. I stopped for a moment and just stared at the blood on his forearm, fearful of moving past that point. I loved this man with all my heart and soul. I continued my slow observation until I reached his face. His left eye was swollen shut, and his face didn't look like that of my husband because of the swelling. I leaned over his body and kissed him on the forehead, my eyes welling with tears.

"I love you. Everything's going to be all right."

"I'm sorry, Mrs. O'Reilly," the nurse said, "but we have to get him prepped for surgery."

I didn't want to let go of his hand; I felt life in his fingers. I wanted him to open his eyes and talk to me. I wanted everything to be okay.

As I sat in the surgical waiting room, our three children arrived. They came over, each staring, afraid at first to ask any questions in fear of the answers.

"How is he?" Ann asked.

"He's in surgery; he suffered a serious head injury," I said.

"Will he live?" my youngest, John, asked.

I slowly looked at each one of them. I could see their father so strongly in their faces.

"I don't know," I replied.

The three of them took a collective gasp. I'd never been so blatantly honest with them about anything.

"What do you mean?" John asked. "This is my senior year; he can't die."

David and Ann sank in their chairs.

"I'm not saying he's going to die. I'm saying that there's a chance he might not make it. I want us all to be prepared for that if it happens."

Strong words, I knew, but I felt like the kids were at an age where they deserved the truth, and if he did pass, we were all going to have to be strong together.

The hours dragged on as we paced in the waiting room. I took turns holding my kids; interestingly, no matter how old your children get, there's nothing that replaces the feeling of wrapping your arms around them. We talked to others in the waiting room, anything to keep our minds busy. Finally, the doctor emerged through the door of the waiting room.

We gathered around him, anxiously awaiting his words. He looked at the floor, then at each of us, and began to speak.

"The next twenty-four hours are crucial. There was a lot of bleeding and swelling. I put in some stents to try to control some of the swelling. At this point, it's a lot of praying. I wish I could give you more."

He turned and left as quickly as he came. I could tell that he didn't think things were going to go well. My two older children picked up on that instantly. My youngest was still holding on to hope.

"That means he's going to be okay, right? Just make it through the next twenty-four hours, and he's home free, right?" John said, eyes wide.

I slipped my arm around his waist and looked in his big blue eyes. "John, we're going to pray and hope for the best."

"Why do you have to be so negative? I believe in my father, and you don't! He's going to make it. He'll be back home, and he'll be just like himself, and I'm going to tell him I was the only one that believed in him." John, crying at this point, ran from the room.

David came to my side. "He'll be okay, Mom." Ann joined us and asked me what I needed. *What I need?* I needed to turn the day back. I needed to fix this. I needed to have someone wrap their arms around me and tell me everything was going to be all right. But instead, I just asked them to take care of John. It was late, so I told them to go home, feed the dog, get themselves fed, and get some sleep.

"Aren't you coming home?" Ann asked.

"No, I want to spend the night here," I said.

"Then so will we," Ann replied while David nodded in agreement.

"No, guys, I need you rested and strong to help both me and your father through these next few days."

They both looked unhappy, but they seemed to understand. They left the waiting room to find John.

It was hours before Joel was out of recovery and in the ICU. As I walked into the room, I noted again that Joel looked quite different. There was a question mark–shaped incision on his head, which had several staples, and a tube going down his throat. A bright-red glow came from a clip on his index finger. The heart monitor blipped like those on TV shows. There seemed to be so many tubes and machines. They had informed me he was on life support because he couldn't breathe on his own.

Joel and I had had the what-if conversation. We had both agreed we didn't want to be kept alive if there was no chance or if there was such severe brain damage we would be a burden. At this moment, our conversation and agreement meant nothing to me. I wanted him back. I didn't care what shape he was in or if I would have to care for him the rest of his life. I just wanted him back breathing; I wanted to be able to touch his body and know there was life there. I didn't care about any on-the-couch-agreement we had made years ago. It didn't count now! I loved him, I wanted him to live, and I would deal with whatever I had to.

As the night wore on, a young dark-haired nurse came on duty, sat, and talked to me for hours. I told her my whole life story. There were very few patients in the ICU, so it must've been okay to engage her in long life tales. She left for a while to check on other patients. Joel started to stir a little, so I quickly stood up and leaned into his face.

"Joel," I said. "Wake up, baby. Joel, please wake up. I need you, and you told me everything would be okay."

Just then, his eyes opened. I saw his blue eyes gazing into mine. It reminded me of how he looked at me the day we got married. The same passion, the same love, I could feel it coursing through me. My heart felt like it was going to pound right out of my chest. I kissed him and tears ran down my cheeks, tears of joy. Then a feeling came over me, as if my heart were getting ripped from my chest.

Joel wasn't saying hello. He was saying good-bye. I could read it in his eyes.

"No, we have too many plans. We were going to travel, and I need your help to do the bills. Joel, you can't leave me. I love you."

His eyes shut, and the heart monitor went to a flat line and one strong, steady sound. People started to run in, and the organized chaos that followed was traumatic. The young nurse asked me to wait outside the room. I knew Joel was gone; he had said good-bye.

I sat outside his room as they worked on him. I was so numb from head to foot that I couldn't even cry. None of this seemed real. I felt like I was living someone else's nightmare. Maybe that's all this was, one of my dreams. I'm going to wake up, everyone will be okay, and Joel will laugh at my dream. I just need to wake myself up from this nightmare. I was shouting, *Wake up!* in my head repeatedly. I stood there, hands clinched, eyes squeezed shut, body rigid, yet I didn't wake up.

The young nurse came, grabbed my hand, and took me to what seemed to be a conference room. A doctor arrived later.

"I'm sorry, Mrs. O'Reilly, but we believe one of the stents gave way in your husband's brain and caused him to go into cardiac arrest. He's being solely kept alive by the respirator. There's no brain activity. Your husband was an organ donor, was he not?" the doctor asked.

"Yes. So wait...you're telling me he's dead, right?" I asked, bewildered.

"For all intents and purposes, yes...he's dead, Mrs. O'Reilly. Your husband had a living will that said he did not want to be kept alive by life support, correct?" There was no hint of emotion in the doctor's voice.

"Yes," I replied. "But don't I have a say?"

"This hospital always likes to support the family through crisis as much as possible," he said, not really answering my question. "We always suggest that all family members be here when the machines are turned off. It helps with closure and the healing process."

Closure—I hated that term when referring to death. Like, if you have closure, it makes everything all right. *Oh, yes, closure heals all*, I thought sarcastically. I felt anger building to rage inside of me.

"So why didn't you put the stent in better? I thought the idea of the surgery was to stop the bleeding!" I shouted, lashing out at him.

"Mrs. O'Reilly, your husband suffered an extreme amount of trauma; he was lucky he was alive when he got to us. Your husband was a fighter; I thought we would lose him during surgery, but he continued to fight." He paused to collect himself, and then continued, "His body gave up, but not his spirit, nor any of the staff at this hospital. We all did our best. I'm truly sorry for your loss."

The doctor stood up. "Call your children; you should all say your good-byes together." Then he turned and left the room.

I sat at my husband's bedside with the last couple of days coming down on me like a boulder, when the exhaustion overcame me. I laid my head down on the bed railing and closed my eyes. I didn't even feel myself drift off to sleep. I awoke, or at least, I thought I awoke.

The room was still the hospital room, but it was warm and inviting, rimmed in a soft white, almost silver-tinged, cloud. I felt safe and rested; there was absolutely no fear, when I suddenly heard Joel's voice, "Hi, babe."

I wasn't frightened by his voice or his presence. There before me stood Joel, goofy grin and hospital gown.

"I knew this was a dream, the accident and all," I said. "I knew I'd wake up, and everything would be fine."

"Sorry, Sara, it wasn't a dream; it really did happen," Joel said.

I was confused.

"So...then...what...uh...where..." I stammered.

"Look," Joel said, "I'm here to tell you that you are special, you have a gift, and you need to use it. I'm fine, and I'm

15

surrounded by love and kindness and spirits who will take care of me. So please don't worry about me. You, on the other hand, were right; you've been called—you have a special talent."

"So, what exactly is this talent and how am I supposed to use it and who exactly should I help?" I asked with an almost sarcastic tone.

"Just like you always wanting to flip to the end of the book to see if it's really worth reading," Joel said with a smile and a chuckle. "You, Sara, are going to have many journeys, and you will discover your talents, and they will grow in intensity, and the spirits will help guide you along the way. You've always been able to help and heal people, but you never really gave yourself credit for what you do, and I never encouraged you because of my own fears. Maybe that's why they let me talk to you, to see you, to let you know there are people and spirits that need you to help and heal." Joel stopped and sighed.

"But I don't heal people!" I said emphatically.

When I think of healing, I think of those preachers that place their hands on the paralyzed or disease stricken and cure them.

"No, Sara, you heal their souls, their spirits. You can make a difference; you can help," Joel said, his voice nearly shouting. He was standing right next to me at this point, looking into my eyes and grasping my arms. His hands slid down both arms to clutch my hands. "Believe in yourself, and follow your heart. I love you," Joel whispered in my ear and kissed my forehead.

The door into the hospital room flew open, and my children entered, followed by a host of family members rushing into the room. I jumped to my feet after being awakened by the influx of people. I was gasping for breath from transporting back to reality too quickly. The sense of well-being was gone, the soft light replaced by fluorescent, the disinfectant odor arousing me like smelling salts.

"Mom," Ann said, "are you okay? What happened last night?"

Before I could answer, the doctor who performed the surgery entered the room. I looked at him, and he knew I was begging for his assistance without uttering a word. He took over and explained to everyone what happened and that Joel was brain dead. He commended Joel for being an organ donor and told us that there would be several people Joel could help with his unselfish donation. I knew the doctor thought this would bring us some sort of satisfaction or comfort, but at the time, it didn't. I stood in the corner listening, watching a sea of emotions come over the room. As the wave unfolded, I saw the different degrees of loss: the loss of a dad, a brother, a son, and a friend. I was frozen as the doctor spoke and took questions; it was almost as if for those few minutes, I was nothing more than a painting on the wall, hanging there for no apparent reason and having no true impact on the environment.

When the doctor left, the wails of my children dislodged me from the wall and threw me into action. All three rushed to my arms, sobbing. Joel's brothers, sister, and mother walked to his bedside, giving the children and me a moment to console each other. As I wrapped my arms around my children, I glanced at Joel's mom, Helen. She had lost her husband at a young age, much younger than Joel actually. Briefly, our eyes met, and a moment of total understanding was conveyed. *What must it be like to bury a husband and a child?* I hope I never know the pain of both, because the one is enough devastation for a lifetime.

CHAPTER 2

LIFE GOES ON

The day of the funeral was one of the most difficult of my life. Yet I felt I had to put up this front of strength for everyone. On the inside, I was anything but strong. I was terrified; I had never felt such fear in all my life. Yes, I was a strong, educated, self-sufficient woman—a frail violet I was not. Or, maybe that's just what I thought. The idea of going through the rest of my life without Joel scared me to death. I was forty-five, but not an old forty-five; I was active, and most people who didn't know my age would never guess I was forty-five. I was lucky that I inherited my mother's genes; she never looked her age either. This was not really an age thing; it was a what-do-I-do-now thing. Joel was not just my husband and best friend; he was a part of me, of who I was—he was my identity.

The service went on forever, and Joel's best friend, Jim, gave a wonderful eulogy. The whole time I was in a state of numbness, glancing from my kids, to my family, to the casket. I tried to focus on the service and what the priest was saying, but it was an uphill battle. My mind kept going back to the dream I had in the hospital room. It seemed so real. *What did it mean?* Again, I wanted to stifle it. It was a much easier way of surviving the moment, rather than dealing with the inner and outer me at the same time.

After the service, we had the traditional funeral potluck at our house with friends and family. What a mistake that ended up being. Our family had tried to convince me to have this at a local hall, but I just wanted to be home. I told them Joel would have wanted it to be that way, even though it really was about me not feeling like going anywhere.

After everyone left, there was a tremendous amount of cleanup. So many people offered to stay and help, but I declined, saying it wasn't a big deal, and I could take care of it. All I really wanted was to be alone. Well, I got to be alone, with a big mess. As the last guest left, I looked at the pile of dishes in the sink and chairs with paper cups and plates sitting next to them that were scattered throughout my house. I turned the lights off and went to bed.

John, my soon-to-be eighteen-year-old son, woke me the next day, crawling onto my bed with his 6′3″ frame taking up the length of it. John was known for his soft-heartedness, but he hated when anyone would refer to him that way. He thought being looked at as kind might take away from his tough-guy persona. As a senior, it's all about being a cool, big man on campus, of course.

"Good morning, Mom," John said softly, as he inched himself up his dad's side of the bed.

I opened my eyes and blinked several times to gain focus. I looked at John and then the clock. It was 11:48 in the morning! I had not slept that late since I was a teenager. I was always an early-to-bed, early-to-rise kind of person, a habit spawned from growing up on a farm.

"Good morning, John. Am I dreaming, or did I actually sleep later than you?"

This brought a huge smile to his face, something I hadn't seen for a while.

19

"Ann, David, and I cleaned up for you. We even vacuumed under the chairs where nobody sees," John said proudly. My children thought vacuuming there was the biggest waste of time ever.

"Thank you so much, John," I said, smiling approvingly. The kids knew how much I hated waking to a mess; my last thought before I drifted off the night before was that I was going to wake to a disaster of a house. My next thought was that I didn't care. It really was a great gift.

John and I lay in bed for a few minutes; he put his arm around me and gave me a manly hug.

"I love you, Mom."

I wanted to cry, but I held back. I didn't want to take away from John's protective moment. If I had done that, he might always be afraid of consoling or protecting, thinking he might always make me or any other female cry, even though that's probably what would happen. At his age, he had years to learn those reactions and emotions.

"I love you too, John. I'm not sure what I would do without you kids," I said.

I always refer to them as my *kids*; now they're growing away from that title, but like it or not, they'd always be my kids. Ann was twenty-three, David twenty-one, and John almost eighteen; they constantly reminded me they're no longer kids. God knows, they'd certainly grown exponentially this last week, right before my eyes, and in my heart.

Joel and I had talked a lot about being empty nesters and what we were going to do to fill up our weekends and summers when there were no more sports or school activities. We acted like we looked forward to it, but secretly I think we both knew we would miss those times. Little did I know I would be looking into the future alone.

As John coaxed me out of bed, I could see that the kids had done a wonderful job cleaning the house. They even made me breakfast, which was a little cold by then, so I suggested we go out for lunch. I love my children, but the last thing I wanted was for them to feel like they needed to spend their time taking care of me. At lunch, I started the discussion about the future.

We went to their Dad's favorite restaurant, which of course brought back so many memories and stories. Everyone took turns telling their favorite story; we basically had our own private memorial service. We laughed until the tears rolled down our cheeks; it was a very cathartic experience. I was so glad we were able to talk about him and not just focus on his death. After we finished, I talked to each of them about their future plans. I wanted them to know, in a very subtle way, that I expected them to continue on with their lives and not think they must dote on me.

On the car ride home, the almost-jovial mood changed; as we passed the corner where the accident took place, an eerie silence took hold—none of us spoke. Ann began to cry. I reached over and took her hand. Still, no words were exchanged; not even gazes were met.

I can't really explain the roller coaster of emotions we all experienced then and in the weeks and months to come. It was like we were all on our own individual roller coaster, processing the grief at different stages with different hills, valleys, twists and turns, feeling nauseated and out of control, wanting to scream, and wishing the ride would soon be over. All I could hope for was that none of us would hit the valley at the same time, as it seemed we did that day in the car. That much sadness in a confined space is too much weight on anyone.

The weeks to follow were filled with legal paper work and trying to get myself and the kids back to our lives. Joel was a planner, thank God. He had insurance that paid off the house and left me with not too much financial worry. He had money in an account to finish paying for David's college and for John's tuition too. We now had the money we always wished for; we could travel and see the world, but one thing was missing—Joel.

As the weeks went on, I was consumed by my dream in the hospital. I would beg to see Joel again. I slept all the time in hopes of dreaming about him, but no dream came. In fact, I seemed to rarely dream. Me! I had always had dreams of some sort. I started to fall into depression. The inner me could barely make it to work and function, but the outer me marched on.

I seemed to be oblivious to those around me at times, especially John. I felt so bad; John was going through so much himself. Senior Night at the end of the basketball season was so difficult for him, not having his dad with him out on the floor as they introduced the parents. I almost felt guilty that it was just me standing at his side. When they announced us, we stepped forward, and John glanced at me for just a second, then back at the crowd. I watched as all the other players showered their parents with hugs and high fives, and I felt cheated, but not nearly as cheated as John felt I'm sure.

At that moment, I realized how incredibly selfish I had been when it came to John and how, as a young man, he must be struggling. Ann and David were older and had somewhat started their lives; they were much more adept at voicing their feelings than John. John was not only dealing with my daily in-and-out struggles, he was dealing with his own. My personal roller coaster ride seemed to be going on a continual downhill track, as I packed on more and more guilt. It was seemingly impossible to try to change my course of direction. I tried to pull it together for John's eighteenth birthday at the beginning of May, but no one was really buying my act at that point. I knew I was drifting, lost in an ocean, and John's anger was becoming more apparent.

The night after his eighteenth birthday, I was awoken by loud noises and what seemed to be yelling. I got up and followed the voices to the kids' bathroom. About halfway there, the air was filled with a very pungent, almost-rancid smell. I heard vomiting and David talking. I peeked around the corner and saw John with his head in the toilet and David sitting on the bathroom vanity.

"Hey, what's up, Mom?" David asked with a bit of a smirk.

"I think I should be asking that," I said.

"Well, young John here thought a chugging contest with Jack Daniels might be a fun thing to do," David said, laughing at his younger brother's predicament.

"I hardly think that's funny, David," I said, a tinge of anger in my voice.

"Hey, don't be mad at me; he's the idiot that did it," David said.

"Well, at least he had the good sense to call you and not try to drive," I replied.

"Actually, it was Missy, his girlfriend, or maybe ex-girlfriend; she was pretty pissed off at him," David said.

"Hey! I'mmmm riiight here!" John said in a drunken slur. "Hate it when people talk about me like I'mmmm not heeeere."

David laughed again and started mocking his brother. "Hate it when people talk about me like I'm not here," David said in a whiny voice.

"Stop it!" John shouted, taking a swing at David but failing to connect.

The movement caused another round of vomiting, which David found uproariously funny.

"Stop it, David," I said in my Mom voice.

"He's getting what he deserves," David said smugly. "You baby him too much," he mumbled as he left the bathroom.

I sat at John's side as the rounds of vomiting continued. I had learned years ago that trying to talk to or reason with a drunk was a waste of time, so I just sat and comforted him, handing him a washcloth when he needed to wipe his mouth.

"I miss Dad," he said, starting to cry.

"I do too," I said.

He turned on me like a viper then.

"No, you don't," he said, nearly growling.

"John," I said, giving him a shocked look. "Of course, I—"

"How would anybody know you miss him? You hardly cried at all; you just walk around like a robot. No one at school could believe you only took a week off after he died. Then…then when you came back, you had a plastered-on smile like nothing had happened. It was weird."

I didn't know what to say.

"John, teaching's my job. I don't want to take my personal issues to work and dump them on the kids; that would be unprofessional," I said.

"Unprofessional!" John puffed. "Listen to yourself! You just lost your husband, we just lost our dad, and you're worried about being unprofessional! I know Dad wouldn't act like that; he would have shown that he cared, unlike you!"

He stared at me with both hatred and hurt in his eyes.

"John, I think that's the liquor talking. You know that I loved your father and I love you kids."

Then I heard the words I'd wondered if any of the kids were thinking.

"I wish it was you who died and not Dad! It should have been you," John shouted through the tears that were streaming down his face.

At that point, David burst back into the bathroom; he must have been in the hallway listening the whole time.

"Knock that shit off, John," David shouted.

He grabbed John by the back of his shirt to lift him up as if he were going to punch him, but he stopped halfway through the movement. David realized John was a sobbing, limp mess, defenseless, so he dropped him to the floor and turned his attention to me.

"Mom, he's drunk. He doesn't mean any of that; he's just an angry drunk," David said.

So many things ran through my head. *Had I been this stoic family figure? Did I come off as an uncaring robot? Should it have been me that died? Would the family be better off? Oh my God, what had I done to my kids?* The room started to spin; I could feel my knees starting to wobble.

"Mom...Mom...are you okay?" David asked.

"See what you've done to Mom, you idiot!" David shouted.

"Leave your brother alone," I said. "I think I better go lie down." I retreated to my bedroom, feeling as though I'd been shot in the stomach with a cannon ball.

The next morning the venomous sting of John's words still lingered. I rose to find David and John sitting at the kitchen table, empty coffee cups nearby. John would hardly meet my gaze. When he did for a slight second, I could see his eyes were swollen and bloodshot. His body language told the tale of his emotionally tumultuous night. His head was slumped between his shoulders, his hands clasped together, arms bent, and elbows resting on the table for stability.

"So, what's my punishment?" John asked.

I poured myself a cup of coffee and walked slowly toward the boys, rubbing my index finger around the rim of the cup.

"Nothing," I said.

"Nothing!" David shouted, jumping to his feet. "What do you mean, nothing?! I would have been grounded for the rest of my life!"

John didn't move an inch, seemingly afraid that if he did he might wake from this dream and I'd change my mind.

"You heard what I said, David, and please don't—"

"Dad would never..." David stopped midsentence when I snapped my neck and gave him *the look*. "I'm sorry, Mom. I'm tired."

"We all are, honey," I said.

I looked at John, who still had not moved from his position.

"John did a very stupid thing; I hope he learned from his stupidity. Punishing him is not going to change what he did. He's eighteen; he has to make those decisions for himself," I said.

David looked at me as if I were sporting two heads but kept his thoughts to himself. I looked at John, awaiting some sort of response, or even movement, but none came. He was frozen by guilt.

"John," I said, "I think you need to go to bed." He rose without saying a word and walked to his room.

David waited patiently, making sure that John had left and his bedroom door was firmly shut behind him before he started the questioning.

"So what's that all about?" David asked with a tone of disapproval.

"What do you mean?" I said.

"You know what I mean. John comes home stinking drunk, says all that mean crap to you, and you let him off." David was still looking at me as if I were from outer space.

"Your brother is hurting. Punishing him is not going to solve anything. When your brother is ready, all I can hope for is that he'll talk to me," I said, trying to implore some understanding from David.

"Don't baby him, Mom," David said.

"I'm not. I'm just trying to guide him through the maze. You don't understand," I said.

David stopped and just stared at me.

"I don't understand? How could you say that?"

"*Ugh!*" I shouted. "I mean, you don't understand what it's like to be a parent."

David waved his hands in the air to stop the conversation.

"Let's just stop the direction this conversation is going in. I have something I really want to ask you."

I was so relieved by the ceasefire declaration. I couldn't handle any more conflict.

"I was thinking about this summer. You know the back-packing trip through Europe I'm doing with my buddies?" David asked.

"Now, wait a minute. You've been planning that forever; you're not cancelling that to stay home," I said.

"No, no, no, that's not what I was going to say at all, Mom. Just hear me out. I was thinking I should take John with me. He needs a break; you need a break. Maybe you could travel this summer too. Something, anything, go on a journey. You deserve it," David said with an inquisitive look.

A journey...isn't that what Joel had said in the hospital? My calling would take me on several journeys.

I sat dumbfounded, David awaiting a response. My lack of words spurred him on with more ideas.

"John and I will be attending the same college in the fall, so it'll give us some time together before we hit the books," David said.

Even in my weakened state, that comment sounded lame; I rolled my eyes. David laughed.

"Come on, Mom. Seriously, you need some time," he said, almost pleading at this point.

"Okay." I couldn't believe that had come out of my mouth.

"But, David...you have to remember to be John's brother, not his dad," I said, cocking my head and looking at him with one eye.

"I know, Mom. When can I tell him?"

"After finals, but before graduation next week."

David leapt to his feet and pumped his fist in the air. "Yes!" he exclaimed.

The next day, I was still reeling from the events of the weekend. I was proud of David for stepping up and wanting to be a bigger part of John's life. David and John had not always been close, but as they started to get older and when David went off to college, their relationship started to change. However, I did have a bit of trepidation about them spending three months together. David so wanted to be the man of the house and take care of everything and everybody. He wanted to be a parent, but I just wanted him to be a son and a brother. He needed to let me be the parent. I did believe, however, that David could provide John with something I just couldn't, male family companionship.

As I meandered through my day, trying to get students ready for finals, I received a note from the office. It said that Principal Sears would like to meet with me after school.

Principal Sears requested I come to his office? Interesting, I thought. It was concerning that I was being summoned without any explanation. Alex Sears and I had always had a good working relationship. I always felt like we were on the same wavelength, which was a nice place to be with your boss, less trouble that way. Sears was a soft-spoken guy with a big heart, and he lived and breathed education. The staff liked his laid-back approach and respected his insight and treatment of their daily needs.

Alex had been keeping a fairly close eye on how I was doing these last few months. He had been so understanding and kind through this whole ordeal. I don't believe a day had gone by since I was back at work that Alex didn't visit my classroom or speak to me in the hallway, asking how I was doing. He truly cared about his teachers and the students. I admired him so much.

"Close the door, Sara," Alex said when I entered his office.

I swallowed kind of hard, thinking, *What did I do?* It doesn't matter if you're a kid, a parent, or even a teacher, that feeling you get when you enter the principal's office never changes. I decided I would break the ice with some humor. Alex and I had a standing comical exchange we had done for years when passing each other in the hall.

"So how's life treating you, Alex?" I would ask.

He would then reply, "Life is great, Sara; it's the people that muck it up."

We would both laugh. It didn't fail this time either and helped put me at ease, a little.

"Sara," Alex said, looking at me and pausing for a bit. "I've been worried about you."

I could feel my face flush with embarrassment. *Why am I embarrassed?* I had known Alex for over ten years; he was kind and considerate. Would I really expect anything less than concern from this man? Logic didn't seem to matter however. I could feel the heat from my face rushing through my veins to the rest of my body. I was starting to sweat, and I hadn't even heard what the man had to say.

Sensing my discomfort, Alex got up from his seat behind his desk and sat next to me in the open chair at the table in his office. He reached over and squeezed my hand, which was resting on the table. It brought back memories of the nurse in the hospital. The rush of emotions was overpowering. I could feel the compassion, the caring, and the sincerity in his touch, just as I had that night in the hospital with the young nurse. In that instant, Alex was no longer my principal—he was my friend. He then spoke to me as a friend, not just an employee. I could feel tears roll down my cheeks and drip off my chin, my embarrassment gone.

"Sara, I know how difficult these last few months have been for you and your family. I worry that you're taking care of everyone but yourself. I really wanted to encourage you to take this summer to travel—get away; go on a journey."

There was that word again: *journey.* Joel said to let the spirits guide me. Little did I know they would come in the form of my son and my boss. Alex went on to tell me what a valued employee I had always been and to ask if there was anything he could do, that sort of thing. He left it with how he wanted to see the old me back in the fall. I guess that was his way of nudging me to get my shit together—I think I needed that nudge. I left Principal Sears's office feeling very different than when I had entered. I felt like I'd just gained permission. But, permission to do what? To go on a road trip? But to where?

That night I dreamed for the first time since Joel's death. I dreamed of a beautiful field with a great big oak tree in the middle of it. The dream shifted many times to different and confusing scenes. One minute, I was in the field, admiring the beautiful tree, then I saw an angry mob, then a sobbing woman, then I saw the face of a frightened young man. The next thing I knew, I was driving past a sign—WELCOME TO MISSISSIPPI—and there stood Joel, waving, and I could read his lips. He was saying to follow my dreams. Beside Joel stood a tall, thin black man in overalls and a work shirt. His lips were moving. I strained to see what he was saying, but I couldn't make out the words.

I awoke, asking myself, *What was that all about? Joel wants me to go to Mississippi?* My dreams were back! Yay! I so loved seeing Joel, even though nothing made sense. I started to let myself drift back into old habits, questioning myself and my ability. I swore I wasn't going to do that anymore. I was determined to ride this journey out and to trust. Trust was a big issue for me. Not so much in other people but in myself. I knew I had to give myself to this process. I closed my eyes; I could feel the room spinning. I felt self-doubt and fear leaving my body as if something or someone were reaching into me and removing all the clutter from my soul. I felt safe, warm, and without fear, as I had in Joel's hospital room that day. I could see the silvery white cloud swirling around me. My heart raced—I was sure Joel was coming back to speak to me. Through the haze, I saw the tall, thin black man, just standing, looking around as if he were searching for someplace to go.

John and Ann pounded through my bedroom door without warning. I leapt to my feet, shocked by being brought back to reality so abruptly. Ann was mad, and it didn't take an investigator to see her rage was targeted at John.

"Mom," Ann said, "would you please tell graduation boy here that, *yes*, he does have to help set up for the party."

"Why? It's my graduation party, my day. Why should I have to work? I'm the man of the hour," John said emphatically.

"John." I groaned. "Would you please do as your sister asks; this is a team effort, and you're the one that's going to benefit the most from this little get together." I glared at John through one eye.

"Yeah, I guess you're right," he said, chuckling a bit. I knew he was just trying to get under his sister's skin.

They both left as quickly as they had entered. My heart was still pounding from the dream, the vision, and the sudden interruption. With all that, I felt like I was going to have a heart attack. It was nearly a massive coronary. As I sat on the edge of my bed, I took a deep breath, trying to gather myself. Disappointment started to sink in; I felt cheated that I didn't get to see Joel. I wanted to see him walk from the white cloud as he had that day in the hospital. Yet the disappointment quickly cleared, and I felt light and happy, as if someone had shaken an Etch A Sketch, creating a new slate to work with. I felt at peace for the first time in a long time.

I entered the backyard and saw that Ann, David, and John had been very busy. All the tables and chairs were set up for the party. John was on cloud nine since David had told him that he would be going to Europe with him for the summer. John was almost giddy with excitement, if it's possible for an eighteen-year-old to be giddy. Whatever it was, it warmed my heart to see John happy again, to see all my children happy. As I scanned the backyard to take in all the work the kids had done, my eyes stopped in shock. There by the tree stood the black man from my dream! Then he was gone. I gasped and stumbled back a few steps. David, seeing what happened, ran to my side.

"Mom, are you okay?" he asked.

Knowing that I would just sound crazy if I told them, I tried to make a joke out of it. "No," I said, holding the back of my hand to my forehead, as if to simulate fainting. This, of course, brought the other kids running.

"I just can't believe I'm getting this much work out of all three of my children at the same time," I said, smiling mischievously.

With a collective gasp, they started swatting at me with feigned slaps.

"Don't scare us like that," Ann said.

"Not funny, Mom, not funny at all," David said.

"No bueno," John said.

The guests started arriving, and the party seemed to be a huge success. Everyone commented on how good it was to see me back to my old self. I started to realize how out of sorts I must have been, but it didn't bother me because, for the first time in a long time, I felt good. Free of any self-doubt or concern, I knew I had a purpose. I continued my mingling with guests, but then I saw the man again. I didn't physically react this time; I just stared for a moment, and then he was gone.

The breeze through the trees seemed to whisper a name: *Jo…si…ah.* "Josiah," I said aloud.

I quickly glanced around to see if anyone noticed me blurting out a random name for no apparent reason. Luckily, everyone was immersed in conversation. *Is that his name? What's his story? How can I help him?* I thought.

I didn't allow myself to question what I was seeing or hearing; I knew it was real, if only to me. Gone were questions of sanity or stability. The only question that remained was where was this journey taking me, and what was the goal?

The next few days were busy—seeing the boys off and explaining to the kids how I had decided to take a road trip to the South and packing. The kids thought I was crazy, but I explained that the region had always fascinated me, and I had an old college friend who lived in Jackson.

"The South in the summer," exclaimed Ann, "have you lost your mind?"

Although the kids had their concerns, they were supportive and thought it would be good for me to get away for a while. So, with their blessing, I prepared for my journey.

CHAPTER 3

ROAD TRIP

I waved good-bye to David and John as they stood in the security line at the airport. John had a grin that stretched completely across his face; he was so excited. David gave him a brotherly punch, and John rubbed his arm, laughing. I was so happy that they were doing this trip together, even though I still had my motherly twitches about safety. I felt in my heart that Joel would be looking out for them.

Ann and I walked out of the airport with our arms linked together. She turned to look at me, her long blond locks falling over her cheek. She pushed her hair behind her ear and said, "I'm glad you're getting better, Mom. You really had me worried."

"I'm so sorry I put you through all that, but I feel much stronger now." I smiled and tightened my grip on her arm. "You know...I never could've made it through these past months without you kids."

"Dad would be proud of us, I think," Ann said, lifting her chin, strength in her voice. "We became a solid team."

Ann and I drove home, chatting about her summer school job and my impending travel to the South.

"So, where all are you going besides down to see Claire?" Ann asked.

Claire was my college roommate; she had lived in Jackson for the last ten years.

"Oh, there's so much I want to see; it's hard to decide where to go first," I said, skirting the question and not giving a definite answer.

I had not a clue where I was going. I didn't want to worry Ann, so I just threw things out, like exploring the South and its history. She seemed satisfied with my answer for the time being. I did wonder how, as time went on, I was going to explain my actions.

My bags were packed, and I was ready to go. Not exactly sure where that might be, I had packed for all occasions. My Honda Pilot had at least half my wardrobe, a sleeping bag, and a tent shoved in it. Although I really didn't think I'd have the courage to camp by myself, I felt like I should be prepared. I had a huge ice chest full of food and drinks, enough to survive for at least a week. Ann looked at the mound I had accumulated and laughed.

"Just where are you going, and how long do you plan on being gone?" she asked. "It looks like you're going on an expedition through the West Indies." Ann grinned at me.

I'm sure she was enjoying this—especially because when we had traveled cross-country as a family, we had only allowed each kid to take one small bag. Her Dad and I had preached efficiency.

"I just want to be prepared," I said.

"For what? Total isolation from civilization," she said with a chuckle.

"No, not *total* isolation," I retorted sarcastically.

Ann smiled, put her arm around me, and said, "It's all good, Mom. I'm just giving you a hard time. Just go and have fun."

A strong sense of freedom coursed through my body. I felt ready.

The next day, I was off. I kissed Ann good-bye, then watched her fade in my rearview mirror. I tuned my radio to a morning newscast and listened to the current happenings. The trial involving the shooting of Trayvon Martin in Florida was all over the news. My heart went out to that poor boy's family. I couldn't even imagine what it would feel like to lose a child. My mind then went to all the young men in my classes that could have been Trayvon. The boys loved wearing hoodies, thought it was cool. That's what life's all about at that age: looking cool, fitting in, being accepted, and not wanting to look like you're conforming.

So many people look at high school kids like they're scary. They're not scary; they're just kids trying to figure life out. Add color to the mix, and people think they're scary gangster kids. It just made my blood boil. Even in 2012, this was still a country with race issues. It totally boggled my mind.

As a teacher and a parent, when tragic, unjust events happen to kids, it felt like it was one of your own kids, a student or family member. In the scope of things, weren't they all our kids? Should we not all be taking care of our children, our future? Maybe that's the problem—we've lost the ability to care for our people. Our society has become self-centered and unconcerned.

I was jolted out of my philosophical daydream by a loud pop, followed by *thud...thud...thud.*

Are you serious, a flat tire?

I maneuvered the SUV to the side of the road. I got out to see what was left of my tire. It was a hot June day, and changing a tire was not something I enjoyed doing, but I was totally capable. I began to unpack my car to get to the spare.

While I dug through my bags, cursing myself for bringing so much stuff, a beat-up, old Chevy pickup pulled up and parked behind my car.

Out jumped a young man, wearing a tattered pair of Levi's and a plaid shirt with the sleeves cut off.

"Need some help, ma'am?"

"That's okay. I've got it covered," I answered.

The young man looked at the ground as if I had offended him.

"I'm not looking for you to pay me. I just thought I could help," he said.

"Oh no! I didn't think you—"

"I'm no shakedown artist or nothin' like that, lady," he said, a tinge of a Spanish accent in his words.

"No...no...I'm sorry. Let's start over. I'm Sara. What's your name?"

He smiled. "I'm Jose. I just live down the road a bit with my family. We train horses," he said proudly. "So can I help?"

"I would love it if you would," I replied.

As the afternoon sun beat down, Jose changed my tire and, in a matter of fifteen minutes, told me his whole life story: His family emigrated from Mexico, and he came from a long line of very successful horse trainers. His mother made the best tamales in the world. His sister married a man from Denver, and they have two kids. His brothers had all stayed near their home. Jose joined the army out of high school and spent some time in Iraq.

I don't think I said two words the whole time; Jose just rattled on without any prompting from me. The tire was changed, and he helped me pack my belongings back into the car. I closed the hatch and turned to Jose to thank him for his help. As I faced him, I saw how truly young he was—jeans that were worn through the knee and grease stained, hands that had seen a lot of hard labor in a short life, but a smile that would light up a room. If people were to judge Jose by appearance alone, they might shy away, thinking he was an undesirable individual instead of a kindhearted young man.

Jose asked where I was headed. I told him Mississippi. A little voice in my head was asking why I'd tell a stranger that much information. Although...I felt safe with Jose, almost as if I had known him for years.

"I spent some time in Mississippi," he volunteered.

"Really, what part?" I asked.

"Oh, outside of De Soto National Forest. I worked on some of the paths in the park."

"Wow, that sounds like a cool job," I said.

Jose looked at me and chuckled a bit.

"Well"—he paused for a second, looking at the ground—¬"I was part of a prison crew. The prison was close to the park, and I was on the good-behavior team. So they let us work in the park." Jose watched for my reaction.

I could tell he wanted to see if my attitude toward him would change drastically. A smile came to my face, and I said, "Well, that beats working on the chain gang."

He was shocked by my response and broke out in uproarious laughter.

"You're right about that, ma'am," he said, still laughing.

He told me how after he got out of the army, he followed a girl to Mississippi. He thought she was the love of his life, but her father didn't like him. Evidently, her father had some political ties and was able to maneuver charges of trespassing, theft, breaking and entering, and assault against Jose.

"All they saw was a Mexican trying to get with some rich white girl and steal from her family," Jose said with distaste. "I didn't do any of that stuff, and Cheryl, that was my girlfriend, Cheryl said nothin' to defend me," Jose said, hurt and anger in his voice.

I felt such a connection with Jose. I assured him that he would someday find the woman of his dreams. He smiled again, showing off his gold-capped eyetooth. I got into my car, and he shut my door for me.

He smiled and said, "Everything's going to be all right. I hope you have a safe journey."

The comment struck me, and I stopped and stared at Jose, not quite knowing how to respond. "Thank you," was all I said.

I drove just a few feet and looked back in my mirror to see Jose—but I didn't see Jose. I saw Joel standing there, waving at me from alongside the road. I slammed on the brakes, and Jose ran to my window.

"What's wrong?" he asked.

I couldn't answer. I just stared at him. After a couple seconds, I regained my composure and asked, "Where again were you in Mississippi?"

"Larksburg," he said.

"Thanks again for all your help; it was a pleasure meeting you, Jose."

"No problem," he replied.

Again, I started to drive away, glancing in my rearview mirror to see Jose waving good-bye. I continued down the road, periodically looking back, breathing a sigh of relief as I peered back a final time, and Jose and his pickup had seemingly disappeared into thin air. A chill went down my spine. "I'm not losing it! Just trust," I said.

The power of the moment started to consume me, and the tears streamed down my face. I wasn't exactly sure what I was feeling or why. Was it fear? I certainly didn't feel scared. Was it the fact that I just saw the face of my dead husband in that of a twenty something Hispanic man? Well…maybe? Although I knew deep down it was more than that. I was starting to feel the shared internal pain. Not like ouch-I-stubbed-my-toe pain; it was the pain that kept me from taking a normal breath. It was the weight of the pain that Jose described for being falsely accused and imprisoned, the heaviness I felt listening to the pretrial discussion on the radio and thinking of all the Trayvon Martins in the world.

My senses were starting to come alive, and flashes of pictures started to fill my mind. I'd had this happen before but on a much smaller scale. This was like the Fourth of July, rapid fire of scenes, pictures, and events. I saw the man, Josiah; I saw the meadow and the tall oak tree. There were crowds of people, then a sobbing young black woman, then an angry, mean-looking man dressed in a military uniform and a small town in the background. I pulled off the side of the road and pounded on the steering wheel.

"Stop!" I shouted. It was all too much.

I exited the car and went to the back to grab a water and sandwich from the ice chest. I had no idea how long I'd been driving, but I knew nightfall was pending, and if I didn't want to use that tent, I'd better find a place to stay. As I got back into my car, I noticed a big sign: Welcome to Oklahoma.

Wahoo, I thought, *I'm getting closer.*

I drove to the next town and found a service station—I needed to get my tire fixed. A nice sandy-blond-haired boy with an Oklahoma Sooners baseball cap took my tire. He told me of a nice hotel and said I could pick the tire up tomorrow, and they would put it on and take the spare off.

The boy had a cute southern drawl. I loved the manners of the South: the *yes, ma'am* and *yes, sir* that were so common in their interactions. I remembered when my son John had a friend over who had just moved to Colorado from Texas. Joel and I were blown away with the *thank you, ma'am* and *thank you, sir*. Everything was ma'am and sir. We had both looked at John, and I asked, "Why don't you talk to us like that?"

John had rolled his eyes and said, "Right…"

I slept well that night, which was a first for me because I usually never sleep when I'm in a hotel. When I awoke the next morning, it was cloudy and looked like it was going to rain. I drove to the service station to get my tire. As I stood in the waiting room eating a bagel and drinking a cup of coffee, waiting for the tire to be put on my car, I had a chance to think about Jose. I thought about his story and seeing Joel in his face as I departed.

Trying desperately to tie everything together, I knew it all had something to do with my journey. I thought about how Jose had overcome the injustices in his life and didn't seem to be bitter. I wondered if the same thing could happen to me. Could I be as forgiving or as strong? Jose stopped to help me when he could have driven by like everyone else. Jose could have assumed that I would think he was a bad person since he had spent time in prison.

My mind drifted as I thought about assumptions we all too often make based on looks and location—location on the almighty ladder of success, which is an arbitrary place at best. For example, if someone were to look at Jose, they might think he was seedy looking or possibly a troublemaker.

Why?

Because his jeans were threadbare and torn. He had a gold tooth and drove a beat-up truck. Would all these visual cues add up to an unsavory human being? Put Jose next to a senator. The senator has the perfect haircut, beautiful suit, drives an Audi, went to Harvard, and has a law degree. Society would automatically assume that the senator has the better character. The same senator that cheated on his wife, embezzled money from his friend's business, and took money under the table to pass legislation. Our society's character meter needs to be based on content instead of on image.

Ding, ding. The bell chimed as a customer ran over the service station cable indicator. The young man with the Sooners ball cap came out with my keys in hand.

"Here you go, ma'am," he said in his drawl. "We got 'er all fixed up fer ya." He smiled as he handed me the keys.

"Thank you," I said, taking the keys.

"It be out back; youse want me to pull it around fer ya?" he asked.

"No, that's okay. I can get it," I said.

I walked out the rear door and turned to see where my car was parked. As I headed toward my car, a strong gust of wind hit. *Swoosh.* The receipt I was holding took flight. I chased it down, stepping on it to stop it from traveling any farther. As I reached down to retrieve it from underneath my shoe, a chill went down my spine. I looked up and saw the tall, thin black man standing by the rear of my car. I stopped, just staring, recalling seeing him in my backyard. The wind again created a voice—*Jo...si...ah*, it softly whispered, as if the trees were calling him.

I did it; I took the leap and spoke. "Is your name Josiah?" No movement came from either of us. I was frozen. I could feel my legs and feet, but I couldn't make them move.

Then I heard the young man from the mechanic shop shouting, "Ma'am, ma'am!" He was coming out the back door.

I turned to face him, wanting to ask him if he saw the man by my car.

"You forgot yer coupon; youse can get a free twelve-point inspection."

I took the coupon and turned back to face my car. The man was gone, disappeared.

"Are you okay, ma'am? Youse look like youse seen a ghost," he asked, obviously concerned.

"I'm fine," I said.

"I's can fetch you some water; do youse feel faint or somethin'?"

"No, I'm fine, just a little tired from the road."

"Well, youse take care, and stop by on yer way back, and we'll take care o' ya."

"Thank you again," I said as I headed toward my car.

As I sat in my car, taking in what had just happened, I asked myself, *Am I really ready for all this?*

Chapter 4

Claire

I pulled into Jackson late in the evening, very tired from the drive but extremely excited to see Claire. Claire and her husband, Alan, had come to Colorado for Joel's service but couldn't stay long. Alan had to be back to work to close a big business deal. I had a hard time understanding Claire's attraction to Alan. He was tall, skinny, had a pointed nose and ears, and in my opinion, was a pompous ass. He had a business-finance degree from Oxford, which he continually threw in everyone's face. Alan, who was never wrong, gave the impression that he merely tolerated the rest of the population, because no one could ever be on his level. Joel had detested Alan, and every time they would visit, Joel would always recommend that we go to the movies, so he would at least have two hours when he wouldn't have to hear Alan speak. I have to admit there were times when I just wanted to smack that needle-nosed stork in the face.

Claire was my best friend in the entire world, so if she loved Alan, I guess I had to keep from smacking him. Although, there was a time about seven years ago when I got a glimpse of the not-so-annoying side of Alan; it was during Claire's breast cancer diagnosis and the treatment that followed. Alan didn't leave her bedside. He gently cared for her and counseled their three sons beautifully through what was a very difficult and scary time.

As I watched him gently stroking Claire's hair, I had thought, *I'll be damned; he is human...*

After that, I tried my best to cut Alan some slack, even though he didn't make it easy.

When I first roomed with Claire at college, I thought for sure we would never be friends. Claire was the studious type, into clothes, and straitlaced. I, on the other hand, was a jock, a little wild, and couldn't care less about fashion. I think when we laid eyes on each other, we both had looks of horror on our faces—me with my long, straight black hair, tennis shoes, shorts, and ragged T-shirt, and her with her big hair, stylish pantsuit, and meticulous makeup. Little did we know that we had just met our other halves of the human puzzle. I've always believed that alone we're just single pieces of a puzzle. It's not until we meet others and join pieces that we realize we need those other pieces to complete our picture. Claire, Joel, my kids, they were all pieces of my puzzle, and without them my picture would be incomplete.

Claire and I embraced, and the tears started to flow. I needed Claire so much. The kids had been great, but Claire understood on an adult level. Claire and I shared everything about ourselves; she knew things even Joel hadn't. She had always supported me and was the first to say that I had a gift. In college, I had a dream about Claire's grandmother, who had died years before we'd met, and passed on a message to her. Claire had said everything was spot-on, and after that, she was a believer.

Claire grabbed my arm to guide me to the house and barked at Alan to get my bags.

Alan yelled back, "You can't be serious. Have you seen how much crap is in the back of this vehicle?"

I told Alan to just grab my blue bag.

He huffed, puffed, and said under his breath, "What am I, the damn porter?"

Claire was eager to talk out of earshot of Alan.

"I can't wait until I tell you everything I have planned and everyone I've spoken to," Claire said.

"Whoa, Claire. I told you everything in confidence; you weren't supposed to tell anyone," I said, shocked.

"No, no, not like that," Claire said.

I had told Claire everything that had happened before and after the accident. I had even phoned and told her what had happened on my way to Jackson.

Claire told me that she'd gone to a shaman, a clairvoyant, and an angel-card reader.

"I must tell you, Sara, I think you possess every ability that they have," she said, talking a million miles a minute. "I'm so glad that you're finally exploring your talents; it's just sad that it took losing Joel for all this to happen." Claire stopped and looked at the ground, obviously knowing she'd just made a very insensitive comment. "I'm sorry, Sara, but you know what I mean."

"Yes, I do," I replied. I knew I would never have gone on this adventure without the tragic circumstances leading up to it.

Claire rattled on, telling me more information about the spiritual world than I could possibly retain. She acted as if this were all for me, to assist me on my journey. The truth, though, was that Claire had always been fascinated by spirits, angels, and the afterlife. She was always telling me about a new book she'd read or what her angel cards said. Claire was always encouraging me to explore my abilities.

She had a whole itinerary of excursions planned for me, and I must say I liked the information she was giving me. The shaman had told her that I should follow my visions, listen to my angels and spirit guides. And the clairvoyant had seen my journey and its great significance in the past and present. She also said that I was being sent to help free people from their shackles; I was to act as a peace guide.

This was all very overwhelming and somewhat hard to believe. I kept telling myself to trust.

The next day, Claire had decided we would travel to Vicksburg to visit a Civil War cemetery. When I asked why, she said she felt this might fit in with what all of her spiritual people where telling her. I still wasn't sure how any of this fit with helping Josiah or even finding him, for that matter, but I went along with it anyway.

As we entered Vicksburg National Cemetery the next morning, I was awestruck by the two large columns at the gate with gold inlay topped by gold urns.

What a beautiful entrance, I thought.

As we made our way into the cemetery, I felt a heaviness in my chest and tightness in my throat.

Is this feeling from stress? This is the first cemetery I've been to since Joel's death, I thought.

I followed Claire deeper into the grounds. I saw a stone that had an excerpt of a poem written by Theodore O'Hara, entitled "Bivouac of the Dead." I read the words on the stone slowly.

> *On Fame's eternal camping-ground*
> *Their silent tents are spread,*
> *And Glory guards, with solemn round,*
> *The bivouac of the dead.*

The words rang in my ears: *eternal camping-ground, silent tents, bivouac of the dead.*

What does it mean?

I slowly raised my eyes from the stone marker, but I was no longer in the cemetery. I no longer saw the rows of white headstones or the beautiful green grass. Instead, dark-gray skies were overhead where there once was blue, and a thick fog surrounded me. I smelled gunpowder.

The cemetery had been replaced by a battlefield. There were injured soldiers pleading for help. I saw medics running from soldier to soldier, trying to lend aid. The ground seemed to be smoldering and had a stench I'd never smelled before, which penetrated my nostrils.

Then I heard a voice. "What's wrong? You never smelled death before?"

Next to me stood a tall man dressed in a military uniform. I believed he was a Confederate. I stammered, "A-are you t-talking to me?" My voice was shaking.

The man looked down at the stone plaque I was reading just moments before. "Bivouac of the dead," he huffed in disgust. "Does this look temporary to you?" he asked, referring to the term *bivouac*, which means temporary camp.

Still in shock, I couldn't reply. I focused on my breathing, which had become labored. I scanned the field and saw a young man, who was missing an arm, walking around; he seemed to be in shock, but I saw no one running to his aid.

A soldier ran up and shouted, "Captain, we have no more supplies. What should we do?"

Another young soldier was wandering around the field, mumbling to himself about something being his fault. Everywhere I looked, there was pain and suffering. I started coughing profusely.

"I can't breathe! I can't breathe! I need help!" I yelled.

Claire ran to my side. "What's wrong?" she asked.

"Get me out of here. I can't breathe," I cried.

Claire grabbed my arm and started dragging me out of the cemetery. I felt like I was going to die; I was sweating and gasping for air. The closer we got to the gate, the better I felt. When we exited, I collapsed on the ground and cried. I'd never been so terrified in my life. I looked around, and everything was back to normal.

"Did you see that?" I asked Claire.

"See what?"

"The battlefield, the dying soldiers, the captain!" I said, my voice a near squeal.

Claire stopped and stared at me, as if questioning my sanity.

"I saw none of that," she replied. "Sara…are you okay?"

By this time, a couple people had come by to ask if we needed assistance. I told them I'd just had an asthma attack. They went on their way, leaving us sitting on the grass. Claire was dumbfounded. She looked at me and asked, "Has anything like this happened before?"

"Not like that, I felt like I was going to die."

As I sat on the grass trying to recover, Claire was on her cell phone, chattering with who I believed was one of her spiritual leaders. For someone who talked about the supernatural constantly, she sure did unravel quickly when being placed right next to it. I sat there while she talked, trying to understand what had just happened. It was all so real! The sights, the sounds, it wasn't dreamlike at all.

Claire finished her conversation and came back to join me on the grass. Her demeanor was unsettled at best.

She sighed. "Well, I spoke to my angel-card reader and told her what just happened."

She paused for a bit, which prompted me to speak up. "So...what did she say?"

"She said I had two choices: one, take you to the nearest hospital"—Claire looked at me for a response—"Or two, find a mystic named Jacinta."

"Who's Jacinta?" I didn't even acknowledge the first option.

"Jacinta is supposed to be a woman who's visited by angels and deities. She's Jamaican and hasn't been here long. My card reader's only heard of her; she's never made personal contact."

"Sounds great. Let's go. What's her address?" I asked sarcastically.

"That's the problem. There is no exact address, just a general location and description of the building."

"Great, a wild-goose chase fits perfectly into my day," I said, continuing my sarcastic tone.

"The good news is that it's not too far from here, and I have a fairly good idea of the location," Claire said.

As we drove, the silence between us started to become painful. I broke the silence with a question.

"Claire...back there at the cemetery, did you see anything? Hear anything unusual?"

Claire, not taking her eyes off the road, said, "I was just walking along reading the names on the gravestones. My back was to you the whole time, up until I heard you yelling for help." Her eyes met mine for a brief second. "So no...I didn't hear or see anything, but that doesn't mean I don't believe you."

"Do you think I'm crazy?"

"You are the sanest person I know, Sara. That's why I'm scared shitless right now."

I usually laugh whenever Claire swears, because it's so unlike her, but I didn't laugh this time.

After driving up and down streets for what seemed like hours, Claire said, "I think this is it!"

She pulled up in front of a dilapidated green stucco building in what looked like a broken-down neighborhood.

"Are you sure?" I asked.

"Yes, green building, spiritual-guidance neon light in the front window," Claire said.

"Are you sure about this, Claire? This woman is supposed to talk to God, and she hangs out here?" I said with a chuckle.

"Yes, that's what my card reader said."

"Well, there's a comforting endorsement," I said, trying to be funny. Claire rolled her eyes at me.

We exited the car slowly and walked to the front door. In the window next to the neon light was a sign that said BUY ONE INCENSE, GET THE NEXT ONE FREE. I stopped, looked at Claire, and said, "What are we doing, Claire? This place seems like some hippie-voodoo shop."

She smiled nervously. "I'm sure everything'll be okay."

I pushed the door open, and the bell chimes hanging above rang loudly, making our presence known. There was not a person in sight. The store reeked of incense and what might have been a bit of weed too. The store was very eclectic; it had everything from Saint Christopher medals to pipes.

Mystic my ass, I thought.

Through a curtain of beads, a large vibrant woman emerged from the back room. She did seem to be Jamaican, at least her attire was. She wore a beautiful bright-green-and-yellow dress with matching head wrap. Her eyes were simply amazing; they were green surrounded by the purist white I had ever seen in anyone's eyes. Her skin glowed surreally, like an airbrushed magazine cover.

"Ah…yuh finally here, mon," the woman said.

"Excuse me, we're looking for Jacinta," Claire said.

The woman laughed and said, "I an I."

"Are you Jacinta?" I asked.

The woman laughed again and said very clearly in her strong Jamaican accent, "Ya, child, I be her. I been feelin' yuh for days now, wondered when you'd finally get here."

Claire looked at her and said, "Did my card reader, Elaina, call you?"

"No, child, I ain't got no phone. I been feelin' dis one for a while now," Jacinta answered, pointing at me. "Now yuh go on, and wait in di car. I have a lot to talk about wid dis one here," she said, looking at Claire.

"In the car…wait out there…in the car, you mean?" Claire said nervously.

"You'd be fine; just lock di doors. Everyt'ing going to be ah-right, mon," Jacinta said, scooting Claire out the door.

Claire looked back over her shoulder at me, seeming like she wanted me to do something to help her. But at this point, I was all in. I needed to hear what Jacinta had to say.

As Claire exited, Jacinta locked the door behind her, which sent a chill down my spine. She directed me through the beaded curtain to the room in the back. I took a seat in the only chair, which was located in the center by a table. The room was dark and cold with storage shelves all around. The hardwood floors looked as if they hadn't been swept for weeks; candles that seemed to be strategically organized about the room provided the only light. A strange feeling of uneasiness swept through me and caused me to feel a bit queasy.

Jacinta started to pace around me, looking at me and shaking her head. Finally she spoke. "Hmm…so you'd be di one. You'd be di special one."

"I'm not sure what you mean."

"Yuh mean to tell mi you'd come all dis way, mon, and you'd still be playin' dis game?" Jacinta said, anger in her tone.

"Game?" I said, puzzled.

Jacinta's demeanor changed, and she became outraged. She paced, got in my face, and flailed her arms around, scolding me as if I were a child. "You'd say I want to help people, yet yuh hold back. You'd say I don't understand mi abilities when deep down you'd know what yuh have."

"But...but..." I tried to interrupt.

"Don't yuh talk now, mon; yuh listen. You'd be a coward—that what you'd be!" Jacinta exclaimed as she pointed her finger in my face.

"I'm no coward. I'm here," I said with strength and conviction.

"Oh, yes, you'd be here, still not knowing if yuh want to believe, still not knowing if yuh want to serve, acting like a scared little pup, that what you'd be," Jacinta said.

"I admit that I've held back for years, not really wanting to believe...not wanting to think I was different, but don't mistake that for not caring or being a coward," I said.

"Believe! Believe! Mon, does dis look like a church? Dis not about belief; dis go past belief...dis faith, mon. Belief, dis what yuh all go to church for...faith, dis what yuh survive on, dis what yuh reach for and feed on, dis what so many have lost," Jacinta said, hanging her head.

I was getting a little confused. "So religion...faith in religion and God, is that what this is all about?" From the reaction I received from Jacinta, that question was obviously a stupid one.

This sent her into another tirade. "Ugh! How could it be dat yuh were given such a bright light and have such a dim bulb?" she said, punching my skull with her index finger. *Okay...wrong there*, I thought. "You, child...yuh have di light...yuh a keeper of di light. Yuh can git vision and give vision; yuh can light a path where only darkness once was. Only yuh blocking di light; yuh blocking di faith," she said, lowering her voice and eyes. She turned to me with a stern look on her face. "Yuh must let go," Jacinta said, almost pleading. "Just let go. Yuh allow fear to drive everyt'ing about yuh! Mon, those fears going to take yuh unda, and yuh never come back someday."

"Fear...what do you mean, fear?"

"Mon, yuh have a shawt memory. Dem spirits in di cemetery, mon, dem were just playin' wid yuh, and what did yuh do?" Jacinta asked.

"How did you know what happened there? Are you sure you didn't talk to the card reader?"

"Yuh still don't git it! Yuh still question instead of knowing, how yuh can squander yuh talents by having a lack of faith, being so scared, not letting go!" Jacinta yelled. "If you'd be not careful, dat fear will come in di form of a very bad man, and he will take yuh to di evil; he will hold yuh down so yuh don't ever breathe again! He takes di light keepers!" Jacinta said, slamming her fist down on the table. "He takes di light keepers, and he neva lets dem go." Jacinta's eyes were bulging, her fist still planted on the table.

The slamming of her fist seemed to knock something loose in me. I looked at the floor for a long time, then up at Jacinta. Her eyes were no longer white; they had become bloodshot from the strain of the conversation.

"You're right…I do live in fear, of myself and the un-known parts of me. Can you help me?" I asked, my voice quivering.

"Child, it's not for mi to help; it is for yuh to see. You'd be the one that holds di light; you'd be the one dat can guide di souls. Believe in di gifts God has given yuh. Listen to yuh angels, and follow di guides that have brought yuh forth," Jacinta said. She hugged my head, then cupped my face in her hands and stared into my eyes. "Yuh must yell to di skies that yuh are ready to serve and believe in yuhself and what di angels tell yuh. Fear is yuh enemy; faith is yuh ally." She slowly released my face from her hands.

"So, what's next?" I asked.

"You'd have more ability than anyone mi evah seen be-fore, child. Don't you'd be wastin' it, discover it, nurture it, and be grateful." Her eyes glowed as she spoke and stroked my hair.

"I've been seeing visions of a man named Josiah," I said.

"Yes…I knows," she said, looking somewhat solemn.

"What can you tell me about him or what I should do?"

Jacinta put her hands on the arms of the chair and bent down a few inches from my face. "Dis is yuh journey, child. Faith is yuh partner. Show courage; let go of all dat has held yuh back. If ever yuh feel fear getting di best of yuh, call on di archangel Michael; he will help protect yuh," Jacinta said with a confident smile and a wink.

Jacinta left the room and came back with a simple cross, carved from wood, strung on a beautiful gold chain. She placed the necklace over my head and again cupped my face in her hands, drew me close, and kissed my forehead. She mumbled some words in a language I didn't understand and released me.

"You'd know what needs to be done; yuh will learn to trust God. Now be on yuh way; di journey awaits yuh," Jacinta said.

Jacinta walked me to the front door and unlocked it. As the door opened, I saw that Claire was no longer alone. A group of young men had surrounded the car, pounding on the windows. Jacinta yelled at them, "You'd be on yuh way, and leave dem alone now, mon."

"Oh, Jacinta, wi just be havin' a lickkle fun wid di white lady," one of the men replied as they all laughed.

As I got into the car, Claire looked like she was the one who had seen the ghosts. "What in the *h e* double hockey sticks took you so fucking long!" Claire screamed at me.

This time I did laugh at her swearing. Claire never used the f-bomb—she must have been really scared.

"I'm so sorry for leaving you alone, but Jacinta, I believe, is who I have been searching for my whole life."

"Well, I hope so, because I just spent the last thirty minutes being terrorized by the local thugs." Claire was still in a bit of a huff.

"Just drive, Claire; I have so much to tell you."

CHAPTER 5

LARKSBURG

I was up early the next morning, anxious to be on my way. I knew I must leave to find Josiah. That night, I had dreamed of him in a beautiful meadow with a huge live oak tree in the center. I saw him standing there in his overalls, sullen faced, staring into the sky. In my dream, I walked toward him, but I gained no ground. No matter how far I walked, Josiah stayed the same distance from me. I heard a voice say, "You must find him and bring him home."

When I turned to see where the voice came from, I saw Jose, the young Hispanic man who had helped me with my tire, standing beside me.

Again, Jose said, "You must find him and bring him home."

I awoke and sat straight up in bed. Larksburg, Mississippi—that's where I had to go. Jose had spoken about Larksburg. I was starting to feel what Jacinta was trying to make me understand. I knew I had to let go of the fear of not trusting my instincts. I felt a new confidence; strength arose in me—both mentally and physically.

By the time Claire and Alan awoke, I had packed and was sitting at the kitchen table, coffee in hand. Claire came out in her blue-satin robe, yawning, and said, "My…aren't we the early riser."

"Old habits die hard," I said. It always drove Claire nuts in college that I was up at the crack of dawn.

I had decided I would wait until Alan left for work to tell Claire I was leaving. Not that Alan would care if I left or not, I just felt like it would give Claire and me a chance to speak freely about what happened yesterday and my travel plans. Alan came dashing into the kitchen, dressed in his three-piece suit, grabbed a cup of coffee and a danish, kissed Claire good-bye on the cheek, gave me a shoulder hug, and was out the door.

"Wow, he sure is talkative this morning," I said to Claire, smiling.

"He has a big meeting this morning, and he was pretty worked up about it," Claire responded, shrugging her shoulders as if it was business as usual.

"Well, I hope you slept last night, because I sure didn't," Claire said.

"I slept great. In fact—"

"I was thinking," Claire interrupted, "I should take you to the shaman today; maybe she could provide some new perspective on this."

"Claire…I'm leaving."

"Leaving! What do you mean? I had plans! You can't leave!" she said, perplexed.

"Please try to understand. Something happened to me after talking to Jacinta. I'm not sure I can even explain it…but I'm different now. I understand myself a little more, and I'm anxious to learn even more and to continue this journey. Josiah came to me last night, I saw him again, and I have to find him to put this all together." I stared at Claire, almost pleading for approval.

She looked down at her coffee cup, disappointment on her face. "I guess I just thought we could do this together. I fantasized about the two of us finding Josiah and unlocking the key to your gifts. I wanted it so badly. Nothing exciting ever happens in my life. It's just the same old thing day in and day out. Sara…you give me excitement, joy, and something to take me away from the mundane. I guess, secretly, I've always wanted to be you." Claire looked up with tears in her eyes, which nearly broke my heart.

I grabbed her hand, looked into her eyes, and said, "I couldn't have done any of this without you. You are my rock; you've supported me for over twenty years."

"Then take me with you," Claire said.

I sighed heavily. "Claire, I can't, and I can't even explain why. I just know that I have to do this alone. Please know that while you may not be with me in person, you are always with me. You are part of me, Claire. You have to know that!"

She began sobbing. "I just so badly wanted to be part of this," she said through a steady stream of tears.

"You are! I promise I will call, text, or email you about everything that happens. Please, Claire, I can't stand hurting you…I'm so sorry…try to understand."

I could tell the shock of my departure was beginning to wear off, and Claire started to gain control. She wiped her eyes and blew her nose; the sobbing had stopped. She looked at me, smiled, and said, "I swear, if you miss one day calling me, I'll be the one sending evil spirits after you."

We both laughed.

"Thanks for understanding. I love you so much," I said.

"And I you. So you better not do anything stupid and get yourself hurt," Claire said, grasping my shoulders and shaking me. Her grip was so tight that it actually hurt.

"Ouch," I exclaimed.

"You deserve it," Claire said, smacking me across the upper arm with a friendly swat. Then she asked me where I was going.

"Larksburg, Mississippi," I said.

"Larksburg! You're going to Larksburg?"

"Yeah, what's the big deal?" I asked.

"Nothing, I guess, but you should know that that place is really stuck in the past. Larksburg is the centerpiece of historic plantations. If you want to visit the past and old-school Mississippi, you'll definitely find it there. Just don't expect a warm welcome. I don't think they take kindly to strangers."

"How do you know so much about it?" I asked.

"My Pilates instructor has a friend who lives there, and she's always telling us about the racial tension there and how everyone's so strange. She also told us some bizarre stories about the town, sounded pretty eerie."

It can't be that bad, I thought. *She's just exaggerating so I'll take her with me.*

"I could get the woman's name and number so you have a contact when you get there; I guess she operates a gym or dance studio or something like that," Claire said.

"Sure, that would be great. Just text it to me when you get it," I said.

I wanted Claire to feel as much a part of this whole thing as possible, so I wasn't going to turn down anything she offered. Besides, having someone, anyone, to get in touch with would be comforting. Claire seemed happy with being able to help; the signs of her dismay nearly disappeared.

As we finished loading my car, we talked about routes to take and time frames. I could still feel Claire's disappointment though. I opened my car door, climbed in, rolled down the window, and looked at Claire. We both had tears in our eyes.

"You know how much I love you, right?" I asked.

"Yes," Claire responded.

I reached out the window for a hug, and we held each other for a long time.

"Please don't take any risks or do anything stupid," Claire pleaded.

"I won't. I promise."

I slowly backed out of the driveway, staring at Claire as she waved good-bye.

I was on the road, and I was excited. It was a beautiful day, and there was little traffic, so I cruised right out of Jackson. I was at a stoplight when my phone rang. I looked down; it was Claire.

Already, I thought. *I've only been gone twenty minutes.*

"What's up? You miss me already?"

"Of course I do, but that's not why I called. I phoned my Pilates instructor and got the name of her friend in Larksburg."

"Great," I said.

"Her name's Margret May, and her studio is at 1517 Main Street. My instructor said she's incredibly nice and that she'll call her to let her know you're coming."

"Thanks so much, Claire. I really appreciate you doing that," I said.

"Anything for you, my love." She chuckled. I was so glad Claire could joke around and wasn't too depressed about my departure. "I think I'm going to call her too. Is that okay with you?" Claire asked.

Not wanting Claire to feel left out, I said, "It would be great if you would do that for me." Claire and I shared good-byes again and hung up.

Still driving, I laughed when I thought of the name Margret May.

Maggie May, I thought, *like the song.*

Right then the radio played the old Rod Stewart tune. A little shiver ran down my spine, but I thought, *I know the spirits are with me on this one. I've always liked Rod Stewart.* I smiled.

My fears were subsiding. I no longer questioned coincidences or insightful thoughts or feelings. I felt confident I was heading in the right direction, and my angels would take care of me and guide me. As I drove, I let my mind drift, examining all that had happened from the day Joel died up to hearing "Maggie May" on the radio.

While I was driving, I passed the prison where Jose said he did time. I imagined what that must have been like for him—a young kid who served his country, only to return to a hateful bigot putting him in jail. Yet, Jose hadn't let that ruin his life. He was angry about the injustice, but he chose not to let that anger fester. He chose to help people, to care and share. I wondered if I could have done what Jose did, or if I would I have lived a life of distrust and anger. Jose had truly forgiven; he had let go of all the negative, hateful feelings. He hadn't granted absolution to his perpetrators most likely, but he had given himself the gift of a normal life by letting go of hate.

I finally came to the off-ramp for Larksburg. I continued down a two-lane blacktop road and saw a sign: LARKSBURG 40 MILES.

I was so excited; I had butterflies in my stomach. On the side of the road was a food stand that sold fruit and fresh vegetables. I pulled over to get a much-needed break and try out some of the local produce.

I walked to the stand and was greeted by a young man who I guessed to be around sixteen years old.

"Howdy, ma'am. May's I help ya?" he asked.

"Yes you may. What do you recommend?" I asked, smiling.

I could tell he loved me asking his opinion, as a huge smile came across his face.

"Well, I reckon I'd recommend these here blueberries and the blackberries. They'd be my favorites, but we also have some mighty-nice taters," he said. I smiled at his southern drawl and his eagerness to help me. "Is you a Yankee?" he asked.

I laughed. "A Yankee…well I'm from Colorado, so I'm not sure what that would make me to you."

"I think that makes you a Yankee," he said in a matter-of-fact tone.

"Really…I guess that's a good thing for me to know," I said, tongue in cheek.

"You bet it is down here. That's a big deal, but I can tell I can trust y'all, 'cause I just know these things," the boy stated.

"Well, thank you. What's your name?" I asked.

"I'm Bubba Jones," he said proudly.

I thought this might be the first in a long line of Bubbas I'd meet on this trip.

"I'm Sara," I said.

"Nice to meet ya, ma'am. So what brings ya to these parts?"

"I'm just traveling, thinking about spending some time in Larksburg," I said.

"Larksburg! What would anyone want to go to Larksburg fers?" Bubba asked.

"Why? What's wrong with Larksburg?" I questioned.

"It's haunted, that's why. They hung black people there, and their ghosts haunt the whole town!" Bubba said, seemingly trying to catch his breath. "They hung people! Have youse not heard of the Larksburg hangin' tree? It'd be world famous!" Bubba's eyes widened as he spoke.

"No, I have never heard of the hanging tree," I said.

Bubba told me the story of this huge old oak tree that was the site of several hangings over the years.

"That tree be like a billion years old," Bubba said.

"A billion?"

"Well, somethin' like that. They killed slaves there, and the Klan would hang black people for just being black. Those people in that town, they be crazy, ma'am. Youse don't wanna go there!" Bubba said, shaking his head.

"So this tree, Bubba, is it still there?" I asked.

"Yes, ma'am, those people have it like a shrine or somethin', and all those..." Bubba trailed off and stared at me.

"All those what, Bubba?"

"My pappy says you shouldn't talk 'bout the dead youse don't know, especially those who were killed by the evil hand. My pappy says youse talk 'bout em, and they'll come an' getcha in the middle o' the night; they just take yer breath away," Bubba said, obviously scared.

"I'm sure it'll be okay, Bubba," I said, patting him on the shoulder. He quickly shrugged my hand away.

"Ma'am, ya don't understand. Larksburg's evil, and evil's powerful. Youse should never provoke evil spirits my pappy says," Bubba said, still shaking his head.

Something came over me then, and I reached out and grabbed Bubba by the arm. I pulled him close, a voice came to me, and I spoke. "Bubba, I promise you that evil will never do harm to you or anyone in your family. Do you understand me?"

Bubba's eyes were as big as saucers. His body was rigid with fear; his eyes raced back and forth across my face.

"What you'd be, lady? What you'd be!" Bubba shouted, backing slowly away from me.

"I'd be a friend," I said as I walked back to my car. I turned, and Bubba was completely still, shocked. I waved, and he returned a slow wave back.

As I drove away, I, too, was in a little shock. I felt a power stirring within me that I had never felt before. I could hear Jacinta in my head, talking to me, encouraging me.

"You'd done good, child; you'd done very good," her voice calmly said.

A smile came to my face, and I knew for the first time in my life that my destiny was at hand.

Forty miles went by extremely fast, and before I knew it, I was looking at a sign that read LARKSBURG CITY LIMITS. I was finally there, and I couldn't wait to see this town. I drove down Main Street and saw that it was still a very old-style town. There were no Super Walmarts here. Only mom-and-pop stores lined Main Street.

Wide concrete sidewalks skirted the streets, and the brick buildings abutted each other; most were two stories. Many of the storefronts had awnings, and some had benches or rocking chairs out front. *Where am I,* Mayberry R.F.D.?

I cruised down Main and saw many people strolling, standing, and talking. This place did not resemble some horror story town. The population seemed to be a mix of races but mostly white. I saw African-Americans walking the streets—not being chased down by white people with ropes and pitchforks as I had imagined. Maybe Bubba had exaggerated a bit, or maybe his father just didn't like this town.

Then I saw a post office at the end of Main Street—next to the post office was an open field. I pulled in front of the post office and parked. My eyes were glued to the field—the field I had seen in my dreams. As my eyes tracked across the grassy meadow, I saw it. The tree...the tree from my dreams. I almost couldn't believe it. I gazed at the biggest tree I had ever seen, which was positioned in the middle of the meadow, enclosed by a wooden split-rail fence. I stood on the sidewalk in front of the post office, glaring at the fence.

"Did y'all come here to see our hangin' tree?" a woman asked.

"W-what?" I stammered.

"The tree? It's world famous, ya know. Did ya come to see it?" the woman again asked in her polite southern accent.

"Ah...well...no. I'm just vacationing throughout the South," I said.

"And you came to Larksburg, Mississippi? How interesting," the woman said in a deep southern tone, sounding almost like she didn't believe me.

"You sure you're not one of those government Yankees that keep snooping 'round down here? Or maybe a *documentary*-type reporter? Is that what you are...hmmm?" the woman asked, looking down her nose at me.

"No...no...I'm not either of those things," I said. I knew, however, that I had to come up with something quickly—before they tarred and feathered me and ran me out of town.

"I'm here to visit Maggie May," I said.

"Oh! That explains it. We love Maggie here. I took her western dance class last week," she said.

Whew...I felt like I had just defused a bomb with only seconds to spare.

"So are you family?"

"No, just a friend." I knew I was lying, but at this point, I was ready to say anything to end this interrogation. Then I thought maybe I should go on the offense.

"My name is Sara O'Reilly. May I inquire your name?"

"Yes, I'm Emma Jean Jenkins," she said, puffing up as though she had just announced she was the queen.

"Nice to meet you, Emma Jean. Have you lived here long?"

"Well, yes I have," she said proudly. She went on to tell me how her family owned one of the founding plantations, and they were pillars of the community.

As soon as Emma Jean took a breath, I started in with a rapid fire of personal questions. "Are you married? Do you have children? Are they educated?"

I could see that she was becoming offended. This was exactly the reaction I was hoping for from Ms. Emma Jean Jenkins.

"You know, young lady, people around here do not like nosey busybodies," she said in a huff. With that statement, she was gone.

Glad to be rid of Ms. Emma Jean, I turned my attention back to the tree. It was hard to believe that something so majestic could be the source of so much pain. As I walked to the opening in the fence toward the path to the tree, I started to feel heaviness—the same feeling I had when I entered the cemetery with Claire. My breath became labored, my heart racing. I stopped. The memory of that day came racing back to me: how I couldn't breathe and felt like I was dying. Feeling a little defeated, I turned around and headed back to the post office.

Inside the post office, a beautiful room with high ceilings, original wood trim, and hardwood floors that shined like they had just been polished greeted me. Immediately adjacent to the door was a community bulletin board with a sign for a room for rent. As I read the sign, I heard a man say, "You lookin' for a room to rent?"

"Yes, I am," I replied.

"Well that one there on the board is upstairs here. It's not the Hilton, you know. Just a bed, bath, fridge, microwave, and hot plate," he said.

"Sounds great. May I look at it?" I asked.

"Sure. Just give me a minute to get the keys." He came back just moments later and asked me to follow him out the side door and around back.

"My name's Arnold Anderson, and I run the post office and own this building," he said, extending his hand for a shake.

"My name's Sara O'Reilly. Nice to meet you," I said. I braced myself for a barrage of questions like I got from Emma Jean Jenkins.

Surprisingly enough, he asked me nothing; he just went on to talk about the apartment.

"It has a private entrance in the back here," he said as we walked up the stairs.

He unlocked the door, and as we entered, I saw that there were two windows, one facing the alley and the other facing the field. I had a front-row view of the meadow and the tree.

"Great view," he said.

"Yes," I replied.

There was a table with a radio on it and two chairs; as he promised, there was a fridge, microwave, and hot plate.

The bed looked fairly old, and when I sat on it, I confirmed my suspicion. In the bathroom was an old claw-foot tub, with a makeshift shower stall in it, and a toilet.

I'm set, I thought.

"Well, what do you think?" Arnold asked.

"How much?"

"One hundred and fifty a month," he said.

"One fifty..." I said in disbelief.

"Yeah, is that a problem?" he asked.

"No...no that's perfect. I'll only be here for the summer. I hope that's not a problem?"

"Nope."

"So when can I sign the lease? And how much damage deposit do you require?" I asked.

Arnold looked at me as if I were from Mars.

"Damage deposit? What...do ya plan on tearin' up the place?"

"No...I just thought—"

"I don't do leases either, too much paper," Arnold interrupted.

I loved how he was a man of few words. I could tell he and I would get along just fine.

"Well, here are the keys. My sister will be around tomorrow to collect the money. Cash—no checks," he stated firmly.

"Your sister?"

"Yes, Emma Jean," he answered.

My heart plummeted to my stomach. "Emma Jean Jenkins?" I asked.

"Yeah, you've met her?"

"Yes, I definitely had the pleasure," I said with a forced smile.

This made Arnold chuckle. "If you met Emma Jean, it was no pleasure," he said as he left the room, shutting the door behind him.

CHAPTER 6

MAGGIE MAY

I arose the next morning to pounding on my door.

"Ms. O'Reilly?"

Knock, knock, knock.

"Ms. O'Reilly?"

Knock, knock, knock.

I rolled over and grabbed my phone to check the time. Eight thirty it read. *I slept in till 8:30!* I was shocked. I grabbed my robe and went to the door.

"Just a minute," I yelled.

I opened the door only a crack to see who it was. There, in all her Sunday glory, was Ms. Emma Jean Jenkins: her strawberry-blond hair neatly done in a big bouffant hairstyle, which had not been in fashion for at least four decades, white pumps, a pastel-print dress that hung two inches below her knees, and a beige clutch that she held onto as if she were carrying a football.

"Good morning, Ms. Jenkins," I said, squinting to avoid the bright daylight.

"Good morning! Good morning? Well, it's almost noon," she said, obviously disgusted.

"Would you care to come in?"

Emma Jean walked in, carefully reviewing everything in the room as if she were checking to see if I had stolen anything yet.

"Well," she said, a huff in her voice, "my brainless brother Arnie said he rented to you! I told him it was a huge mistake. You could be a mass murderer for all we know." She glared at me with one eye.

This made me giggle just a little.

"What do you think is so funny, missy?"

"Ms. Jenkins," I said calmly, "I believe I owe you an apology."

Emma Jean looked a little surprised at my comment.

"When I got into town yesterday, I was very tired from driving, missing my kids, and all that. I know I was rude to you, and frankly, you of all people certainly didn't deserve to be treated in such a manner. I certainly hope, you being a Christian lady and all, well…maybe we could start over today? Maybe we could be friends," I said, as though frosting a cake with my words.

I think I was channeling some southern BS slingers. Although, I knew I did not want one Emma Jean Jenkins as an enemy. So I was prepared to say or do anything to swing her back to my side.

"Well," she said in that huffy voice I was becoming accustomed to and annoyed with at the same time. "You will find, Ms. O'Reilly, that people in these parts use manners. I will admit that I was *fit to be tied* after our first meeting. However, since you have seen the error of your ways, and I am a good southern Christian woman, of course, I will forgive and forget." She smiled one of the most plastic smiles I have ever seen.

I delivered my best mannequin smile and said, "Thank you. Thank you so much. I do appreciate how understanding you are." I think I might have gone a bit overboard on the last part because even Emma Jean seemed skeptical.

She cleared her throat and said, "Well…you're welcome. Now there's the matter of the rent."

"Oh, of course." I went to my bag to get the cash.

As my back was turned, Emma Jean reiterated what her brother had said to me yesterday. "Cash—no checks."

"Yes, I have it all right here," I said as I counted it out, then put it in her hand. "I was wondering if you could tell me where the nearest bank is. I need to cash a check."

Emma Jean looked at me quizzically and said, "It's right next to Maggie May's studio on Main. You did say you were a friend of hers, right?"

"Oh"—I slapped the heel of my hand to my forehead—"of course. I guess I was so tired when I came in yesterday afternoon that I just didn't notice."

"It would behoove you to be more observant next time, especially in this town. Good day." Emma Jean huffed, threw her nose in the air, and closed the door behind her.

After her departure, I realized I had better focus on finding Margret May before Emma Jean discovered I was lying about knowing her. I quickly showered, dressed, and was on my way to explore downtown Larksburg—all ten blocks of the business district.

As I came down the back steps and turned the corner around the post office, I faced the tree. It was as if it, or someone, was watching me. Not just watching but stalking my every move. I stopped and looked at the path that led to the tree. *I'll do that later,* I thought, and turned to start down Main Street.

There wasn't much traffic or many people or cars. It was as if I had gone back in time about forty years. I expected the theme song from *The Twilight Zone* to start playing. I walked by a shoe- and saddle-repair shop, a barbershop, and a bakery. Most of the stores were service oriented. The only thing that might be mistaken as a department store was a place called Woolworth—it was a pharmacy, feed, hardware, and clothing store all in one. It seemed to be the biggest building in town; it was three stories high. I walked around inside it for a while. It was like a mini agricultural Walmart. It had a little bit of everything. I decided I didn't have time to shop; I needed to find Maggie May's studio.

As I walked out of the store, I spotted a huge sign across the street that read First National Bank. Next to the bank, just as Emma Jean had said, was Maggie's dance studio. I crossed the street and made my way to the entrance. As I got to the corner, a small black child, who was barefoot and wearing overalls and a ragged shirt, ran up to me and grabbed both my hands. He could have only been five or six years old. I looked at him and his beautiful face that seemed to glow like an angel.

"Will you help my daddy, lady; will you help my daddy?" the young boy pleaded.

A loud pop went off—it sounded like a gunshot. I jumped and turned toward the direction of the noise, only to see it was a car backfiring.

I turned my attention back to the boy, but he was gone. I looked in every direction—there was no sign of him. *How could he disappear that fast?* I thought. I stood there for a while, trying to see if there was anyone in need of help or to catch a glimpse of the boy again. I saw and heard nothing; people were starting to stare at me. I decided it was time to move on and brushed the incident with the boy aside, although the boy's face haunted me. He was stunning. I know all kids are cute, but there was something so special about this child it was hard to shake him out of my head. However, I knew I had to talk to Maggie May and quick—before Emma Jean had a chance to talk to her.

I was finally at the entrance to the studio; I took a deep breath and went in. There was a small reception desk inside. Pictures of dancers and advertisements for exercise classes lined the wall by the door. The other walls were covered with mirrors.

"Hello...anyone here?"

A woman appeared from the back room. She had a bounce to her step and a smile on her face.

"Hello, I bet you're Sara O'Reilly," she said with a slight giggle.

"Yes, I am. I guess you were warned of my arrival," I said, a smile on my face.

"Boy, have I been...first, my friend Pam who teaches in Jackson called, and then your friend Claire called and kept me on the phone for over an hour," Maggie said with her hands on her hips, but a smile was still on her face.

"Claire...sorry about that. She can be a little overprotective. I hope she didn't bother you too much," I said, grimacing a little.

"No, no, absolutely not. I had a blast talking to her about Larksburg and you and your trip down here."

Thoughts started racing through my mind. I was wondering what—and how much—Claire told this woman. Maggie must have read my mind.

"Don't worry. I know you just met me and know nothing about me, but I assure you, your information is safe with me," she said.

I knew in my heart that Claire wouldn't have said a word to her if she didn't trust her, and I trusted Claire's judgment.

Maggie then told me the story of how she ended up in Larksburg. She was an undergrad majoring in theater and dance at UCLA when she meet her husband-to-be, who was on leave from the army. It was love at first sight. After his discharge, Gary, her fiancé, stayed in California and finished a bachelor's degree in biology.

They married immediately after graduation in a ceremony at a courthouse. Maggie's parents were tragically killed in a car accident when she was in high school, and Gary had never seemed that close to his parents, so they decided to not have a big wedding. Apparently, that had been a mistake—Gary's parents were angry about not being included in the wedding.

Not long after the wedding, Gary's mom called because his father was sick, and she wanted him to come home—without Maggie. Gary explained that she was his wife, and they were a package deal.

"I was so nervous about the move," Maggie said. "Gary hadn't spoken about his parents much, and I didn't pry. I just knew how much I loved him and that I'd follow him to the end of the Earth if needed. The arrangements for the move were made, and Gary got a job teaching biology at the local high school and later became the head football coach. In this part of the country, being the head football coach made him a god, and during a winning season, higher than a god, if there is such a thing." Maggie laughed.

"His parents, and the whole town for that matter, hated me on sight. Gary was somewhat of an athletic legend in the town, and his parents were wealthy plantation owners. Everyone seemed to look at me as if I were some harlot who robbed them of their icon," Maggie said, shaking her head and looking at the ground.

As I listened to Maggie tell her story, I started to feel an overwhelming kinship with her. I could see why Claire trusted her with my story. As she spoke, she never stopped twisting the wedding band on her finger. I could tell she had mixed feelings. When she started talking about how she was ostracized by her in-laws and the community at large, her overwhelmingly positive demeanor turned morose—happy on the outside, yet extremely conflicted on the inside. I could tell that she could be quite the actress when needed; I supposed that's how she survived.

"I am so sorry. Yet you stayed all these years?" I asked, trying to understand how she could take all this societal abuse.

"Yes, I stayed. I was young, in love, and soon to find out I was pregnant with our first child," Maggie said.

She went on to explain that not long after they arrived, she started to figure out that the town of Larksburg wasn't exactly normal in more ways than one, and the hold Gary's parents had over him was suffocating at best. After the baby was born, Gary's father, Clive, made a miraculous recovery from his illness. Maggie believed he was never really sick; it was just a way to get Gary back in their clutches. She and Gary started to fight all the time.

"I was working up the courage to leave—until Clive got wind of it. He kicked his tenants out of this building, remodeled it into a dance studio, and handed it over to me. All he said was, 'Here's something you can do with your time.'"

"Sounds like a real charmer," I said.

Maggie nodded. "I set up classes in aerobics and dance, knowing no one would come. But, Clive put the word out, and when Clive Anderson talks, people listen. I had people signing up in droves; not only were they signing up but they were talking to me also."

"Anderson? I thought your name was May?"

"No, it's Anderson. My middle name is May, but there was no way I was putting that name out front. I know it really pissed Clive off too," Maggie said, satisfaction lacing her voice.

"So now everything's good for you?" I asked.

"It's definitely better—but weird."

"Weird?" I asked.

"Yeah, the women who had spent the last few years avoiding me and whispering about me now came in the studio smiling and hugging me. It was like that movie...you know? What is it?" Maggie said, obviously searching for the title.

"*The Stepford Wives*," I said.

"Yeah, *The Stepford Wives*. Like they were robots...Clive Anderson's robots." Maggie chuckled at the thought.

"If Clive is the town bully, what's his wife like?" I asked.

"Like queen of *The Stepford Wives* club," Maggie said.

With that, we both broke out into laughter.

"Hattie, Clive's wife, and her sister-in-law Emma Jean."

"Oh no, Emma Jean Jenkins!" I exclaimed.

"Yep, that'd be her. A piece o' work, isn't she?"

My face flushed. "Oh no, did Emma Jean tell you we met? I didn't get a chance to talk to you before..." I was almost in a panic.

"No worries, I had already talked to Pam and Claire before Emma Jean started grilling me," Maggie said.

I sighed heavily with relief.

"You really pissed her off. What did you say to her?" Maggie asked.

"It wasn't so much what I said, but more the way I said it. No…I take that back…it probably was what I said. Actually, it was both." I smiled. "But I can explain that later. What did you tell her?" I asked.

"I assured her that we were friends; we meet at a yoga convention a few years ago."

"What was her response to that?"

"She just huffed and said that explained a lot."

Maggie said she then excused herself from the conversation because she didn't know what I had already said to Emma Jean.

"Whew! Thank you so much!"

"You try to steer clear of Emma Jean—and Hattie, for that matter—as much as possible while you're here," Maggie advised.

"Well that might be a challenge," I said.

"Why do you say that?"

"Because I rented the apartment above the post office," I said sheepishly.

"Wow, and Emma Jean knows about this?" she asked.

"As of this morning, she does. Her brother, Arnold, was actually the one who rented it to me, but Emma Jean picked up the rent. She was not exactly happy," I said.

"I bet she wasn't. And I'm sure she let Arnie hear it," Maggie concluded.

"So, what's Arnie's story? He seems nice. I actually think he rented the place to me just to piss Emma Jean off."

"Poor old Arnie. I think someone zapped him with a stun gun when he was born, and he never recovered," Maggie said.

We both laughed again. I was enjoying the fact that we had the same sense of humor.

"He does seem kind of nice, really quiet," I said.

"How would the poor guy ever get a chance to speak growing up with Emma Jean. Besides, I heard he was his father's whipping boy. You know...never good enough, that kind of thing. I think that's why he just stays in the post office instead of running the plantation," Maggie said.

I was so enjoying Maggie's company and conversation that I had almost forgotten why I came to Larksburg. I glanced up on the wall and saw a family picture.

Maggie saw me staring and said, "My husband, Gary, and the two boys—twelve and fourteen now. Hard to believe they're that old. Do you have kids?"

"Yes...but they're older. My daughter's a teacher, and my sons are in college, but they're on a trip in Europe this summer. I miss all of them so much...but I call my daughter every night and either text or email my sons." My voice hung there, waiting for the inevitable question.

"And...are you married?" Maggie asked.

After a long pause, I took a deep breath and said, "I'm a widow; my husband was killed in a car crash earlier this year."

It was the first time I had ever had to say the word *widow* before; it made my heart hurt.

Maggie gasped. "Oh my god, I'm so sorry!"

I could tell the revelation had startled Maggie, and she was scrambling for the right words. I had already gone through that with family and friends so many times. There just are no right words.

I gave Maggie a quick out and started talking about the town and how it seemed to be stuck in a time warp. This made Maggie laugh again, which relieved the tension.

"I hope you don't take this the wrong way, but I have to ask you a question."

Maggie's laughter stopped. "Sure, what is it?"

"Why are you helping me? Don't get me wrong...I feel like we have a lot in common. But you don't even know me. Yet, you've been so open with me," I said, a questioning look on my face.

Maggie looked at the ground for a long time, apparently picking her words carefully before she spoke. When she did begin to speak, a look of determination came over her face. "There's something wrong here...in this town...with some of the people. Now, I don't know if it's that horrible old tree. If it's the atrocities that happened here. But I do know I don't want my boys growing up with the umbrella of evil that seems to loom over this town. It's something I've felt since I came here." Maggie sighed heavily.

"Can you tell me some of what's happened here?" I asked.

"Larksburg was a big Klan town, but before that, some of the old plantation owners here were known for their cruelty to the slaves. As far back as anyone can remember, that big tree— 'the hanging tree' they call it—was the site of many deaths. The people in this town point to it as if it's a national monument or something.

"Anyway, over the years, the stories of strange occurrences and sightings have multiplied. I myself have witnessed some strange things that happen to the tree at night." Maggie paused and took a drink of water.

"Like what?" I asked.

"I've seen that tree glow white, as if spotlights were shining on it, in the dead of night. Other times it glows bright red, as if on fire. Many times, people have called the fire station, only for the firefighters to arrive and everything's back to normal. People have said they've seen the ghosts of the victims of the hanging tree walking the streets at night. There are those who have even said they've seen them during the day. There's one…a little boy…always asking for help for his father."

"A little boy? A little black boy, barefoot and in overalls?" I asked.

"*Yes!* Did you see him?" Maggie asked, her eyes bulging.

"Yes, I did, right before I came in here," I said, looking around, pondering everything Maggie had just told me.

"Like I said, I'm not sure what all's goin' on around here, but I can tell you whatever's at that tree, I believe it wants out."

"Wants out?" I said. "Why do you say it wants out?"

"I don't know why I think that. I guess because…why would anyone want to stay here?" she said, shrugging her shoulders.

"After talking to your friend Claire, I just think you might be the one to set it—or them—free. I just know that for the last couple of weeks, the activity around the tree and in the town has been at an all-time high. I just figured it had something to do with you coming," Maggie said, looking into my eyes for a response.

"You said there was something about the town and the people. Can you tell me more?" I asked.

"Well, it's hard to explain, but there's just an air of evil, distrust, and anger amongst the people here. I even saw it in my husband shortly after our return. I believe Gary even knows it. Gary was born Clive Gary Anderson, but he told me he would never use the name Clive because it was cursed. His dad was outraged when we didn't name either of our sons Clive. Gary said that awful name would die with him."

"So, people…are they just mean to each other?"

"Yes, that's the obvious part, but there's more to it. I swear that sometimes there almost seems to be a fiery red in their eyes. It seems to come and go. I've seen it in Gary's eyes on occasion, and it's frightening. What scares me more is that I'm starting to see it in my boys' eyes," Maggie said, sighing again.

Just then, the door to the studio burst open, and a bunch of giggly teenage girls came storming through.

"I have a hip-hop class to teach right now, but we'll talk more later. In the meantime, the library has loads of information about the hanging tree. You should go by and read up on it," Maggie said as the teenagers converged on her.

I waved good-bye and told her I'd connect with her later. Maggie smiled and waved back as she conversed with her gaggle of teenage students.

CHAPTER 7

HISTORY

I continued my exploration of Larksburg to try to see if I could find the library. As I strolled down the street, peering into windows, I noticed a market. I was starving, so I went in to get some food. I knew the chance of take-out was fairly slim, but I'd take anything at this point. I wandered to the back of the store to the deli section. A sign on the counter said BOX LUNCHES $5.25. A hefty man with a bristly stubble beard and a dirty-white butcher's apron was behind the counter.

"Can I help ya?" he said around the toothpick in his mouth.

"Yes, I was wondering what was included in your box lunch," I asked, smiling.

"Well…it be your basic box lunch: sandwich, chips, dill pickle, po-tay-ter salad, and a Pepsi." He looked at me as if I were an idiot for not knowing such information.

"That sounds great! Could I get a tuna salad on rye?"

The butcher rolled his eyes and answered, "We don't have no tuna salad or rye bread; we gots turkey, ham, or roast beef. White or wheat."

I could tell he was exasperated with me. "Turkey on wheat would be great, and could I get bottled water instead of the soda pop?" I asked.

"No, we ain't got no bottled water, but I can give you a cup, and you can get water from the fountain against the wall. It's as good as Per-ry-air," he said, laughing at my request.

I collected my lunch and water and headed for the exit, all the while listening to the man chuckle at me. As I exited the front of the store, I spotted a bench with a small tabletop. Next to the table sat an old black woman in a wheelchair. She was wrapped in a shawl and blanket, which I found odd since it was at least 90 degrees with 110 percent humidity. The woman also appeared to be blind—she wore small, very dark spectacles. She stared straight in front of her, no head movement, as if there were nothing around her.

"Mind if I sit here?" I asked.

"Sit wherever you want. It'd be a free country, or at least that's what I'd been told," the woman said, not moving.

In silence, I sat, unwrapping my sandwich and trying to think of a good conversation starter, when suddenly the old woman spoke, "So, you'd be the one."

"Excuse me...the one?" I replied.

"Yes'm, the chosen one, we'd been waitin' for you," she said, still unmoving.

This was a little eerie to me, but I knew she had to be someone who could help me unravel myself—not just me, but my purpose.

"My name's Sara O'Reilly," I said.

"I's know who youse are," she said sharply. "Youse know there's been others before you," she said.

"Others?" I questioned.

"Yes'm...others. None had the sight though," she said.

"The sight...do I have the sight?" I asked.

She laughed. "Child, only youse can answer that...have to conquer your fear first," she said, lowering her voice.

Fear...the same thing Jacinta told me. "So what can I do to conquer my fear?"

Again she laughs. "Girl...youse sure have a lot to learn. Where's your faith? Or maybe you'd be 'fraid o' that too?"

It seemed as though everyone talked in riddles, like all this was some elaborate game, but someone forgot to share the rules with me. I was really starting to get frustrated. I knew I needed to get a hold of myself, so I took a deep breath and asked a simple question, "What's your name?"

"Josephine, but my friends call me Josie," she said.

Finally a straight answer. "Do you know a Josiah?" I asked.

"Oh, yes'm, I know o' him," Josie said.

"Can you tell me about him?" I asked.

"Child, youse fixin' to learn a lot 'bout Josiah," Josie said.

A young black teenager appeared from the store wearing a shop apron. "Time to come in, Grandma," he said.

"Your grandmother is a nice lady," I said to him.

The boy looked at me as if I were a mental patient. He grabbed the back of the wheelchair and started rolling her back into the grocery store.

"I would love to talk to her again. Is she out here often?" I asked.

Again the young man just stared at me as if I were crazy. "From time to time," he said.

I so wanted to finish my conversation with Josie, but I knew better than to push at this point. I finished my sandwich and continued looking for the library. I asked a gentleman where the library was, and he pointed me in the direction. You would've thought that I had asked the guy to drive me to the library and carry me in by the angry tone in his voice as he barked out the directions. I didn't know if it was just because I was an outsider or what…but everyone I came in contact with seemed to have an air of anger about them. Be that as it may, I took the angry little man's instructions and headed straight to the end of the block and took a right.

I had walked about half a block off Main Street when I saw a glorious old brownstone building sitting on a huge city lot surrounded by trees. A sign on the corner said CITY LIBRARY AND COUNTY COURTHOUSE. Both sides of the walkway that led to the library were lined with beautiful flowers all the way to the front steps of the building. I grabbed the metal handrail and proceeded up the steps to the two massive entrance doors that had large black-metal handles. As I entered, there was a sign designating where everything was in the building: courtroom straight ahead, DMV to the left, county clerk to the right, library upstairs.

As I started up the staircase toward the library, I was pleasantly surprised when on the door I saw a sign that said Wi-Fi available. *Wow, finally something from this decade*, I thought. I walked to the front desk. There, peering at me, was an extremely petite woman, reading glasses perched on the tip of her nose; she was dressed like a stereotypical librarian from the early 1950s.

"May I help you?" she asked.

"Yes, thank you. I would like to learn more about the tree on the edge of town. I hear it has a colorful past," I said.

"Are you another reporter?" she asked.

"No…no. I'm a teacher that just loves history," I replied.

"Well in that case," she said, looking at me with curiosity for a moment before moving on with her questions, "are you the one that moved into the apartment over the post office, Maggie's friend?"

"Yes…yes that would be me," I said, forcing my lips to smile.

The librarian smiled back, saying, "Oh, I see. If you go to the far-right corner in the back, you'll find all we have about the history of the hanging tree," she said.

I headed to the back of the library, winding through long rows of shelves with books stacked to the ceiling. I felt like I was walking through caverns; it was kind of creepy. I saw a door labeled HANGING TREE MUSEUM.

These people are crazy, making a museum out of what should be an embarrassment! I thought.

Inside the museum, the walls were decorated with pictures that ranged from victims of hanging to the Klan. I slowly walked the perimeter of the room in disbelief of what I was seeing, when I heard a voice.

"Quite the display," the voice said.

"Quite the display of hatred," I said, turning to face the voice.

I was shocked to see an elderly black man with gray hair and slumped shoulders, walking with a cane. The man smiled, paused for a while, and then said, "We must learn from the hatred in order to understand love and forgiveness."

"Forgive all this?" I said, pointing around the room. "You're a better person than I."

Again the man showed his teeth with an almost-knowing smile and said, "To bring kindness and generosity into your soul, you must first combat evil and slay its origin. How else can you embrace love and discard fear?"

All I could think was this guy must be the town preacher or something. "Do you work here?" I asked, a bit of disbelief in my voice.

"Yes...although I consider this more of a labor of love than a real job," he said.

I was now convinced this guy must be nuts. I stopped and studied this man with the kind smile and gentle spirit. I wondered how he could not want to just burn this place to the ground. I'd only been in the room for five minutes and I already wanted to torch the place. As I studied him, he seemed to be doing the same to me. He finally broke the awkward silence.

"My name is Joseph," he said, extending his hand.

"I'm Sara," I said, grasping his hand.

His hand was cold and rough, but warmth spread through my body as soon as we touched. The feeling was so comforting and appealing that I almost didn't want to let go. His smile broadened as the handshake took an awkwardly long time.

"Oh, sorry. Nice to meet you," I said, trying to cover for the oddly long handshake.

"So you're here to learn about the hanging tree?" Joseph asked.

"Yes, I am. But, Joseph, if you don't mind me asking..." I searched for the right words to finish my sentence.

Luckily Joseph saw I was uncomfortable with the question and finished it for me. "How can a black man work in the Hanging Tree Museum?"

"Yes. Aren't you full of anger?"

Joseph smiled again, looked deep into my eyes, and said, "We must learn from the mistakes of the past if we are to thrive as human beings. Evil met with anger and resentment only amplifies evil's power. To conquer, we must learn to release the power of love, not be controlled by fear."

"Are you a preacher or saint or something?" I said jokingly. But to be honest, I really was wondering if he was a saint.

Joseph laughed and patted me on the shoulder. "No, I'm not a preacher nor a saint," he said, shaking his head. "I'm just a keeper of the past and a believer in redemption."

"I guess that's why I'm here…to learn from the past, that is," I said, stumbling over my words somewhat.

"Well…where would you like to start?"

"I'm not sure."

Joseph gave a friendly chuckle and said, "How 'bout we start with the plantations and their owners."

"That sounds good to me," I said.

Joseph then reached to the top shelf and brought down a huge, long book, which resembled a scrapbook. He directed me to a table and chair in the corner of the room. The book was made of full-grain leather, and burned into the cover was "The Planters."

"What's a planter?" I asked.

"They were the plantation owners who owned land and slaves," Joseph said.

Just the thought of the history we were about to embark on made me sick to my stomach. To think other humans thought it was okay to own people and treat them like animals was so hard for me to believe. It happened, I know, but for anyone to think for even a minute that behavior was okay was hard to digest.

Joseph opened the book, which on page one had a map of Mississippi with the different cities written in big, bold print. Joseph pointed to Larksburg on the map and started his history lesson.

"Around here, there were four main plantation owners back in the 1800s, or at least those are the ones we have the most records of. There were several smaller operations, but these four here, they were the big-money landowners," Joseph said, pointing to an extremely old photo of four well-dressed business-type men. "But this one—this one here—he was the one who ran the county. Heck, he ran most of the state of Mississippi." Joseph pointed to the man in the center that was dressed in what resembled a military uniform.

"What was his name?" I asked.

"Clive Anderson, or I should say Colonel Clive Anderson. Everyone referred to him as Colonel," Joseph said, shaking his head.

"Clive Anderson!" I said in disbelief.

"Ahh, you must've already heard of his great-great-grandson," Joseph said, raising an eyebrow.

"Yes, I have. He's the father-in-law of a friend."

Joseph paused, cleared his throat, and said, "People think the present-day Clive is bad, but he ain't nothin' like his great-great-grandpappy. The Colonel was pure evil, the evil that you just know is sent from the devil himself," Joseph said, passion in his voice. "The stories of the things that man did to his slaves would curl your toes. I also hear that he was not too great with his own kin either. Of course, they're just stories."

Joseph turned the page to a picture of the Colonel's family. "Wow, he had a lot of kids," I said, pointing at the family photo that looked like it was taken on their porch.

"Those are just his white children. Hear tell he fathered many a black child, but he only let the boy children live. The girl children he put in a gunnysack and threw 'em in the river, or so people say," Joseph said, gazing at the book.

With that statement, I felt bile rise in my throat. "He did what?" I exclaimed.

"Well, you see, the Colonel only thought the males were worth keeping because he had enough breeders and house people, so he just figured the male children would bring more at market. So, he would just drown the females like a litter of unwanted pups."

I sat back in my chair, taking in what I had just heard. I couldn't even comprehend what that must have been like, to have a baby ripped from your arms, thrown in a sack, and tossed into a river. *How could anyone do such a thing!*

I looked at Joseph; I had no words to express how I was feeling. I could feel my face becoming flushed and my eyes welling up with tears when Joseph reached across the table and grabbed my hand and said, "Don't you start in now; we've just begun, so you best take a deep breath and toughen up now, ya hear."

With that statement, Joseph's grip on my hand tightened, as he willed strength into my body. I nodded my head in compliance and stood up for a moment and shook my arms, shaking off the emotion I was feeling. I sat back down and looked at Joseph.

Joseph looked at me and said, "Are you ready to go on?"

"Yes."

Am I really ready to go on? I thought.

I had obviously read about the atrocities of slavery before. I watched documentaries and studied it as part of my history major in college. I guess all I did was read and watch—I never really connected. I was just another privileged white girl who felt bad about what happened, but I never really understood the true brutality of slavery. Or maybe I never felt the cold-bloodedness as I did that day.

Now with Joseph telling me the stories and showing me the pictures, and just being in Larksburg, I could feel the heaviness of what had happened. It was as if, for short moments, I was transported back as the young slave girl being raped by her master, then having her baby thrown into the river. My feelings and insights were running on an all-time high. I had never felt such pain throughout my body.

I turned to Joseph and asked, "I know this doesn't matter, but I just have to ask. Did the Colonel do this to all the baby girls born on his plantation or just the ones he fathered?"

"You know, that's the strange thing. He only killed the ones that he was pretty sure he fathered. He let the other ones live," Joseph said, shaking his head in disbelief.

"He killed his own flesh and blood. It just doesn't make any sense that he would do it to the girls and not the boys," I said, and then I stopped. "What am I saying—it doesn't make any sense that he would do it at all! It's all evil, just pure evil!"

"Most of what the Colonel did and said made no sense to the normal person. Everyone lived in fear of him. He led a life without love, compassion, or logic. It was said that he killed the girls so he wouldn't have to keep track of which ones were his kin, afraid of incest and all. The Colonel claimed to be a religious man," Joseph said.

"What a pig!" I shouted. "You said he didn't treat his own children very well either?"

"No, he'd get drunk and beat 'em. Some of his boys that weren't mean enough for the Colonel's liking, he'd belittle and berate them in an effort to toughen 'em up. Most of his children, when they got old enough, ran off. Or at least it was said they ran off."

"Do you think he murdered his own children?" I asked.

Then I thought about what I had said—he had *already* murdered his own children.

"Well...it's told that the Colonel would tell people they'd be gone and no one ever questioned him," Joseph said.

Joseph continued to thumb through the book, showing me graphic pictures of torture alongside pictures of people working in fields or sitting in front of cabins. The pictures told a story of an everyday existence that included daily doses of punishment and abuse. My body started to ache with every turn of the page. The pain was becoming overwhelming. Joseph then turned the page to a picture of a slave family: a man and his wife and two small children, leaning up against a hitching post in front of a one-room slave cabin.

"Oh my God! That's him!" I exclaimed.

"You mean Josiah Anderson?" Joseph said.

"Anderson?" I questioned.

"Yes...Josiah was brought to the plantation as a small boy and was given the master's name."

"So he wasn't fathered by the Colonel?"

"No, no...Josiah was two or three when the master won him in a poker game," Joseph said.

"A poker game!" I exclaimed, raising my eyebrows.

"Yes, a poker game. So Josiah never knew who his parents were, but the Colonel always considered Josiah good luck, because he won big that night in poker, basically cleaning everyone out. After that, Josiah grew into somewhat of a trusted slave for the old Colonel. Josiah had to do a lot of the dirty work for the Colonel by turning other slaves in for taking extra food or planning an escape—those kinds o' things."

"Josiah was an informant, a rat?" I said.

"Josiah did what he had to do to survive, for his family to survive!" Joseph barked at me. "Don't be so quick to judge," he added. "It was a very different time than what you're used to. It was about surviving. If Josiah didn't do what the Colonel asked, they would beat him or someone close to him until he complied. So until you know what that's like, don't be so quick to condemn," Joseph said in a stern voice.

"I'm sorry, Joseph. You are so right; I have no idea what Josiah was going through," I said sheepishly.

I was embarrassed by my reaction. I guess I had imagined that Josiah was a leader of the slaves and was unjustly hanged and I was here to free his spirit. I guess that scenario was more about my ego than reality. I could feel myself humbling to my purpose.

With humility setting in, I examined the photo. Josiah's wife was stunning. Even in an aged photo, her beauty was apparent. His daughter looked like she was about eight and his son about four. When my eyes fell upon his son, I felt a sense of familiarity. I stared at him intensely; it was him— the little boy asking for help on Main Street. I gasped and looked at Joseph. Joseph showed no reaction to my obvious recognition of the people in this photo. It was as if he just knew that I knew them. Joseph paused for a short time to allow me to take everything in and come to grips with what I was seeing and feeling.

"Can you tell me about them?" I asked, pointing at the picture.

Joseph just nodded his head and began his story about Josiah. "Like I said, Josiah was a trustee of sorts on the Anderson plantation, but he was also the first slave hung at the now-famous hanging tree."

"But, I thought he was on good terms with the Colonel."

Joseph just laughed and said, "There's no such thing when you deal with evil."

Joseph continued, painting the picture of what Josiah's life and daily routine were like; he spoke about how much he adored his wife and children and how Josiah hated the role that he had to play on the plantation. The other slaves hated him, the Colonel's kids hated him, and the white field handlers hated him. However, his wife and kids adored him. When he was with them, Josiah felt free. The Colonel knew how jealous the others were of Josiah, and he played on that jealousy to make it even more uncomfortable for him. Everything was a game to the Colonel; he loved to manipulate people, anything to cause pain—both physical and mental. Joseph shook his head but continued telling the story.

"One day, Clive Jr., the Colonel's eldest son, who absolutely hated Josiah, called Josiah to the big house to have him help set up for a dinner to which some of the surrounding plantation owners had been invited. Little did Josiah know that Clive Jr. was setting Josiah up to be blamed for some missing silver and cash from the house. Clive Jr. had taken the cash and the silver to pay off some gambling debts. Clive Jr. knew if his father found out, he would beat him, so he devised a plan to blame it all on Josiah."

Joseph paused in his story, almost to heighten the suspense—he had to feel my anticipation, as I hung on his every word. Joseph glanced at me sideways and continued his tale.

"Clive Jr. told Josiah to fetch the silver and china and bring it to the dining room. Josiah started to walk in the direction of the closet, which was referred to as the silver-and-china room, when he noticed that Jr. was not accompanying him.

'Ain't youse comin', master?' Josiah asked. Josiah knew no slave was to be in there unattended.

"'I don't need to hold your hand, you black bastard. Just do as I say,' Clive Jr. replied. Josiah did what the master had ordered.

"Later that night, when the plantation owners and the Colonel had some liquor in them, Clive Jr. informed the Colonel of the missing silver and hidden kitchen cash. Clive Jr. made sure to announce it in front of all his father's friends, knowing his father would have to take drastic measures as to not look weak in front of the other plantations owners. Clive Jr. also knew his father would not dare question his story in front of his friends and neighbors. To risk the possible embarrassment of even slightly insinuating your own son might be in the wrong and a slave right would be unheard of in that day. The Colonel summoned Josiah to the house."

As Joseph continued to talk, I could feel myself almost floating, as if I were going to pass out—the room was spinning. When the room stopped spinning, I was no longer at the library. I was standing on the front porch of the Anderson plantation. I was surrounded by the other plantation owners, and Josiah was being dragged to the front yard. I was there, I had gone back in time, and I couldn't believe it. I naïvely thought I might be able to stop all this from happening.

I ran forward to put myself in front of the Colonel. He neither saw me nor heard me; I reached out to grab his lapel, but I couldn't grab any cloth. *Am I only here as an observer?* How cruel of a situation. The Colonel walked by me and spoke to Josiah.

"Josiah, was you in the silver-and-china room today?" the Colonel asked.

"Yes'm, masta, I's was," Josiah responded, his eyes racing wildly with fear.

"Was anyone with you?" the Colonel asked, anger in his voice.

"Nos, sir, no ones wit me," Josiah said, hanging his head, anticipating what was coming.

"Well you know, boy, you ain't never to be in there alone?" the Colonel said.

"Yes'm, sir, I's knows, but—"

"See, Daddy, I told you," Clive Jr. interrupted, sniveling.

I walked over to Clive Jr., just wishing he could see me or hear me say, "You're a needle-nose little prick, Clive Jr."

With a nod of the Colonel's head, two of his hired white hands grabbed Josiah, stripped him of his clothes, and chained him spread-eagle between two poles. The Colonel slowly walked around Josiah.

"So, you stole from me, boy, after all I've done for you," the Colonel said, slowly stroking the handle of a leather whip.

"Nos, sir, nos, sir. I's never steal from youse, sir," Josiah said emphatically.

"So, now you're not just a thief, but you're a liar too," the Colonel said.

"Nos, sir. I beg youse, sir. I ain't steal from youse, sir," Josiah said.

I screamed, even though I knew no one could hear me, "Please, don't do this!" As I pleaded, I looked at Josiah's scarred body; he'd obviously received brutal beatings in the past. How could anyone withstand such a series of abuse?

With a snap of the whip, the first lash cut into an old wound on Josiah's back that ripped open. "Where's my money and silver, boy?" the Colonel demanded.

"I's don't knows, masta," Josiah cried.

The beating continued with the same question asked and the same anguished response from Josiah. Then Josiah screamed out, "Master Clive Jr. he's tells me go in myself, sir."

That statement brought rumblings from the crowd that had gathered. I heard some of the people whispering about Clive Jr. and how he was the one who probably took the silver and the money. The Colonel overheard the accusations, sending him into a rage. The Colonel's eyes turned black as he barked at his hired hands to get a chained neck collar and place it on Josiah.

"Okay, boy, let's go pay a visit to your wife and kids; maybe they can help us find my property."

I could tell even Jr. was getting nervous at his father's rage.

The white handlers dragged Josiah's naked, beaten body down a path to the slave quarters. They bound his hands and feet and hung the neck chain over a tree branch to hold him in place. Josiah's wife and children stood in front of their home looking helpless and scared.

The Colonel looked at his son and said, "Okay, go in there and find the money and silver."

"You know, Daddy, he probably already spent it or hid it in the woods or somethin'," Clive Jr. said, sounding panicked.

"Well, go in there, and make them tell you where it is, son," the Colonel barked .

"Okay, Daddy." Clive Jr. tugged on one side of his pants and then the other, as if that would help him be a bigger man.

Josiah started to scream and beg for the safety of his family. "Please, sir, youse can do anyt'in' youse want to me, but please, sir, don't harm my family," Josiah pleaded.

Clive Jr. turned to a couple of hired hands and waved them to come in with him. The men grabbed Josiah's wife and kids and threw them into the cabin. We heard the screams and wails of his wife and children, the sound of glass breaking, and saw the horrific image of Clive Jr. through the window, pressing Josiah's wife against the wall and ripping her clothes off. She screamed and cried as Clive Jr. raped her in front of her children.

I dropped to my knees. I was helpless. I couldn't do anything. The men laughed and whooped and hollered at Clive Jr.'s actions. Clive Jr. came out the front door, adjusting his pants and smiling at the reaction of the crowd.

"I didn't find noth'n', Daddy, and I looked in every hole," Clive Jr. said, laughing. This brought more cheers from the crowd.

Josiah's anger overflowed, and he glared at Clive Jr. and shouted, "I'll kill you, Clive Jr."

The crowd turned dead silent.

"I'll kill you," Josiah screamed again, his eyes bulging with rage.

"Did you hear what he said, Daddy?" Clive Jr. said.

"Yes, I did, son," the Colonel said, glaring at Josiah. And without blinking an eye, he looked at his hired hands and said, "Burn it."

"Nos, sir, please. Nos, please," Josiah screamed.

Josiah's wife and children tried to escape the cabin, but they were pushed back in, and a board was nailed across the entrance. The hands lit the cabin on fire, and screams mixed with smoke bellowed out of it. Josiah's faced swelled with pain.

The Colonel turned to Josiah and said, "You never threaten an Anderson." He yelled at his hands to get the buckboard and horses. "I'm gonna make an example out o' you, boy, so the whole town can see," the Colonel said.

The crowd followed the buckboard to town, to the large live oak tree by the post office. It was clear at this point that Josiah didn't care what happened to him. Everything that meant anything was gone. They strung a noose around Josiah's neck and placed him on a horse. The Colonel slowly walked the horse forward, as if savoring every moment. Surely the Colonel wanted him to beg, but Josiah just stared straight ahead. The Colonel called Clive Jr. over and whispered in his ear, "Son, you and your gambling just cost me a prized slave."

Clive Jr.'s eyes widened in shock as he looked at his father. The Colonel just stared at Clive Jr. as he pulled the horse forward. With the snap of the rope, I was jolted back to the reality of the library.

Joseph was still talking as if nothing had happened. He finished his story by saying that the Colonel would not let anyone cut the body down until the smell and sight was offending the whole town. I kept blinking my eyes trying to figure out how all this happened.

Just then a voice came over the intercom: "The library is closing in five minutes. Thank you for exiting."

Joseph looked at me and said, "It's getting late. You should go home; we'll talk again."

I stood up without saying a word and walked to the exit. The librarian smiled and said, "Come again."

I had no response. I walked out to the bathroom beyond the doors of the library, entered the stall, and commenced vomiting.

CHAPTER 8

JOSIAH

I awoke to a glorious sunrise and the sound of children playing on the sidewalk under my window. I had thought I wouldn't sleep at all after the experience I had at the library. I was pleasantly surprised, however, by falling asleep quickly. I'm sure it was out of total exhaustion. Once I was asleep, Joel came to me in my dreams and comforted me as only he could. He had a way of holding me that made me feel like everything was going to be all right, no matter how dire the situation seemed. I had missed that feeling of security so much since his passing. I melted into his arms as he whispered in my ear that everything was going to be okay and he was proud of me. All the horrifying events of the day had disappeared with his touch.

I felt strangely rejuvenated and confident this morning. I made coffee and started my day. *My day...*I wasn't exactly sure what I was going to do. *What's next?* I sat at the table, drinking my coffee and gazing out the window at the hanging tree. I kept replaying what had happened to Josiah, thinking how awful it was and wondering how many others had met the same fate. I picked up my phone and read several texts from the boys and Ann. They all seemed to be doing so well. The boys were having a blast in Europe, saying it was the trip of a lifetime. Ann was content with teaching summer school.

My phone rang. It was Claire. *Oh no*, I thought, *I forgot to call her.* I knew she was going to be pissed. I answered with an exuberant, "Hi, Claire!"

"What the hell, Sara! You promised you would call every night!"

"I know, I know. I'm sorry. It was a really rough day, and I came home and just crashed," I said.

Her tone switched from angry to inquisitive quickly. "So what's happened? Do you like Maggie? I really like her. How are the townspeople? Are they weird?" Claire was asking so many questions I could barely keep up.

"Hold on, Claire. I'll tell you everything; just be patient," I said. The other side of the phone went silent, and I could feel Claire's anticipation.

I started at beginning of the day with the boy and meeting Maggie May. I agreed with her about Maggie. Claire was uncharacteristically quiet; she seemed to hang on my every word. I told her everything about the library, the Hanging Tree Museum, and being transported back to witness the tragedy of Josiah's death. When I finished, I was exhausted from reliving it. There was a long pause, and I could hear Claire crying.

"Claire, are you okay?" I asked.

No answer—just sobs.

"Claire, did I go too far in my story? I know it was brutal. Maybe I should have left some stuff out, but you said you wanted to know everything."

"No! I'm glad you told me. I think I had just romanticized this whole journey you're on. I was even jealous at times. Now I see it differently. It's all more...real," she said softly.

"I know what you mean. Yesterday changed my life forever," I said. "You read and study about slavery and oppression, but it's not *actually real* to us. Yesterday I felt so white, stupid, and privileged, all at the same time."

That made Claire laugh. "It sounds funny, but it's so true."

"Yes, another unfortunate truth," I said. I heard a knock at my door. "I have to go, Claire. Someone's at my door."

"Okay, don't forget to call!" Claire yelled into the phone.

At the door stood Ms. Emma Jean, a piece of paper in her hand. "Well, good morning, Ms. Jenkins," I said. Emma Jean pushed by me and walked in. "Come right in," I said.

Emma Jean turned sharply as she caught the sound of sarcasm in my voice.

I quickly changed my tone, reminding myself I did not want her as an enemy. "My, you look nice today, Ms. Jenkins. To what do I owe this pleasure?" I asked, smiling.

Emma Jean paused, looked around again, obviously trying to spot anything out of the ordinary. She turned her attention back to me, looking me up and down. I was still in my pajamas; since I was on the phone with Claire for so long, I hadn't had a chance to get dressed. "Oh, so sorry"—I looked down at my pajamas—"I'm having a lazy morning."

"Hmmm, well I'm just here to give y'all a receipt for your rent," Emma Jean said.

I was sure the receipt was just an excuse to come up and make sure I hadn't destroyed anything yet.

"Well, thank you," I said.

There was a long, awkward pause. Then Emma Jean looked at me, tilting her head, and said, "So, I hear you spent all afternoon at the library, poking around asking questions about the hanging tree. You sure you're not one of those reporters?"

"Nooooo, not me. I'm just a history buff," I said.

Emma Jean did her patented *hmmmmm*, followed by a huff. "Well, I'll be on my way," she said.

I closed the door behind her and was relieved her visit hadn't lasted very long. I changed my clothes and returned to my coffee and granola-bar breakfast. I really needed to get some groceries. I turned on the old radio that was on the table; the knob for the tuner was broken, but it seemed to be on a station that played just enough mix between news and music. The music ran from oldies to rock and country—all the music I loved. It also played the Reverend Al Sharpton's news show; he was covering the Trayvon Martin story.

As I listened to the radio, I gazed at the hanging tree, wondering exactly how far this country really had come with race issues. I thought of how scared the boy in Florida must have been. I remembered the look of total fear on Josiah's face as he watched his wife and kids burned alive. I pounded my fist into the table and looked to the ceiling.

"Why, God, why? How could you allow these atrocities to happen?" I shouted.

I guess I needed someone or something to blame, and God was an easy target. I thought back to catechism classes and how the priest would make statements like *God has his reasons* or *God does things that we do not understand; we just must have faith.* I remember thinking then, *Why all the mystery?*

I decided it was time to go for a walk and visit the tree. I realized I'd been avoiding it since I'd arrived. I could hear Jacinta's voice in my head, telling me not to be afraid. I knew that fear was holding me back in so many ways. I had to ask myself, *Why? What am I afraid of?* The spirit of Josiah needed me; for whatever reason, Josiah hadn't moved on in the spirit world, and I had to figure out why.

As I approached the tree, I felt that same choking sensation I had that day in the cemetery. I stopped for a moment and swallowed hard. *Not this time*, I thought.

When I reached the base of the tree, I said, "Josiah, I wish to talk to you." Right then a swift breeze blew though me. It was like being hit in the stomach—it hurt. It was Josiah; I just knew it was Josiah.

"Josiah, I'm here to help you," I said.

"Help me...help me...?" a voice said. Josiah then stepped from behind the tree and walked toward me. He was dressed in a white peasant shirt and ragged pants, his feet bare. His nostrils where flaring with anger, and his eyes pierced me.

"Youse think youse can help me?" Josiah asked in a hostile tone. "Youse expect me to think that God gonna sends a white woman to help me!"

"I'm not sure my skin color is the issue here," I said.

"*Youse skin color is everything!*" Josiah said in a growl.

This is not at all what I had expected. I thought he would be glad I was here; instead he resented the hell out of it. Josiah continued to pace around me like a wild beast ready to pounce on its prey.

"Josiah, I know what happened with the Colonel," I said.

"Youse hush up! Youse don't know noth'n'!" He stopped pacing, looked at me, and asked, "What you'd be? One o' those psychics? Or maybe a messenger from God." Josiah laughed. "They'd all been heres, ya know. For all kind o' reasons, and they *all* gots *scared off.*" He seemed confident with his last statement.

"I don't plan on being scared off. And as far as what I am...I don't really know, but I know I want to help you," I said.

Josiah laughed again. "Youse think youse can help me!" He pointed at the ground. There at my feet was a mound of hair. "Oh my God!" It was my hair! I touched my head and felt only skin. I screamed and ran away from the tree, holding my bald head. I ran as fast as I could back toward the post office, hearing Josiah laughing in the background. I saw my reflection in the post office window—all my hair was still on my head. I ran my fingers through it as my heart pounded a million beats a minute, tears streaming down my face.

I saw Arnold near my side by the post office entrance. He didn't say a word about my obviously bizarre behavior. He just shook his head and walked inside.

I stood outside, glaring at my reflection, reassuring myself that I wasn't bald. I couldn't figure out why Josiah was so mad at me; I meant him no harm. I wanted to help him find peace.

Josephine, I thought. *I need to go talk to her; she might be able to shed some light on this.*

I headed down the street toward the market, hoping she'd be perched outside. As I got closer, I saw that she was indeed sitting outside, wrapped in her normal attire. I was so excited I almost broke into a jog. I sat down next to her and waited for a group of people to leave before I spoke.

"Josephine!" I said.

Before I could ask anything, Josephine laughed. "Youse been havin' a bad-hair day, child," she said.

I was stunned. "How did you know about that?" I asked.

"Oh, child, when you gonna learn this ain't just 'bout you?"

"Okay...so it's not all about me; but why is Josiah so hostile toward me?" I asked.

"Child, youse ever listen to yo'self?" Josephine said in a disgusted voice.

I paused to think about what I'd just said. I let out a heavy sigh. "Obviously, I don't listen to myself. I just want to help him."

"*Why* youse wants ta help him? For youse? Or fer him?" Josephine asked.

I paused again and thought. "I had never really thought of why I was doing what I was doing. I just knew I was compelled to do it. I don't really believe it's specifically about Josiah or me anymore. I believe it's about a purpose...I feel. A purpose that's guiding me toward something bigger than myself," I said.

Josephine smiled; it was the first facial expression I'd seen on her face. "Child, youse may gots what it takes."

"I still don't get it. I really don't understand the connection. I'm still confused," I said, almost pleading with her for guidance.

"Josiah's hurtin'. He wants to go on and bes wit his kin, but he's can't. His spirit's trapped here, en it won't let 'im go. You gotta helps him accept love and reject his fears. You gotta helps him find God's peace," Josephine said.

"How am I supposed to help him? When I try to talk to him, he does stuff like make my hair fall out."

"Child...spirits, de don't play fair. If youse give 'em fertile ground to plant fear, de bes' gonna do it! You gotta have faith that God's gonna care for ya, that he'd bes in charge. Youse gotta have faith in de gifts God's given youse. If youse do that...God'll give ya peace, the kind o' peace that'll see ya through all attempts to shake ya," Josephine said. Josephine's words alone seemed to bring me peace. It was like going to church without going to the building. I stared at Josephine as she continued her straight-ahead posture. She seemed to glow, or maybe it was just my feelings toward her at the time, feelings that reflected like a mirror— it gave me a sense of peace.

"Trust yo'self, child; let go o' all your fears; don't give 'em noth'n' to latch on to," she said. Josephine's grandson appeared again to wheel her back into the store. This time, the boy said nothing, just stared at me again as if I had three heads. *Teenagers*, I thought.

I sat outside the store, reflecting on what Josephine had said—especially the part about letting go of my fears. I thought back to when Claire had cancer and was going through chemo. Walking into her hospital room and seeing her with no hair terrified me. Embarrassingly, I wasn't terrified for *her*—the thought that someday that might happen to *me* was what had gripped me. I remember feeling guilty about being so selfish and self-centered. Claire saw the look of horror on my face, and I could tell it was devastating to her. I never got over letting Claire down like that, being so weak in character. Claire and I never spoke of that moment, which I believe made it even worse. It's a regret I'll always carry.

I realized what Josephine was saying about letting go of fear. I could see how Josiah only had to scratch my surface a little to get me to crumble. *Never again*, I thought. If I was going to do this, I needed to give up whatever perceived power I had and put my trust in the spirits that had guided me here.

I decided to go back to the library to visit with Joseph more; I felt like the more I learned, the better insight I would have into Josiah.

As I passed the librarian at the front desk, she said, "You sure don't look like you've been stung by bees."

"What?" I replied, confusion most likely lacing my features. "I'm just here for more research."

When I entered the museum, Joseph was in the rear filing books. He looked up and greeted me with a smile. "Hey, you're back. I thought I might've scared you off for good," Joseph said as he walked toward me.

"No, not a chance. I'm in for the long haul," I said without hesitation.

I could tell that Joseph was pleased with my confident reply.

"So, what brings you here?" he asked.

"More information," I said. Joseph cocked his head back and gave an approving nod.

"If you don't mind me asking...what's your intent with all this information?" he asked.

I paused for a second, thinking. "I'm trying to help someone."

"Help someone how?"

"By making a connection of sorts, I guess."

"How will this connection help this person?" Joseph asked, as if he already knew the answer.

"By helping them find their way home."

Joseph beamed. "I can see you have learned a lot since we last spoke."

"That I have, Joseph...that I have," I replied, smiling.

"Well then...where do you want to start?"

"I'd like to learn about other people that were victims of the tree."

Joseph again went to the shelf and brought down a large leather-bound book, except this one had a white cross on the cover. I reached over and outlined the emblem with my index finger.

Joseph watched with curiosity and then asked, "What?"

"Joseph, I know we don't know each other, and this is an extremely personal question, but may I ask what you believe?"

"What I believe? You mean, religiously?"

"Yes...do you believe the fire and brimstone and that everything in the Bible is fact? That kind of thing?" I almost felt embarrassed at my question.

Joseph smiled and reached across the table, grabbing my hand. "I believe we all hold within us great power to either fuel the good and douse the evil or vice versa, and, yes, I believe that was put in us by God. Why do you ask?"

"I guess because I never thought of myself as a church-going religious type. I've always been a spiritual person, believing there was a Supreme Being; I never had a problem referring to that as God or angels. I've always believed we follow a path through this world and into the next. I guess my belief is what's seen me through the death of my husband. I know in my heart of hearts that I'll see him again someday."

"So what's the problem?" Joseph asked.

"I guess I'm having some self-doubt, feeling a little inadequate. Feeling like maybe some mistakes have been made by choosing me."

"Choosing you for what?" he asked.

"Never mind. I'm just talking nonsense," I said, shaking my head.

Joseph gripped my hand tighter and said, "Whatever you've been chosen for, I'm sure God knows what he's doing." I smiled. I was so grateful for the vote of confidence Joseph had given me and the power he shot through my veins by the mere touch of his hand.

It was still hard for me to believe I was on this journey. I'd never viewed myself as someone with low self-esteem, but I never saw myself being given a privilege like this. I really considered this whole situation an extreme privilege—to be able to serve others, to help bring peace to a situation—it was a thought beyond my grasp. I always told my kids that with privilege comes great responsibility. Little did I know I'd be living that statement.

Joseph opened the book. There on the front page was a list of names: Josiah's being the first name on it. Next to the names were columns for age, date, crime committed, and notes.

Crime committed—what a joke! I thought.

Next to Josiah's name was *theft and disobedience.* The list included almost 50 names, and the dates ranged from 1835 to 1952. I took my index finger and started down the list. It was hard to believe anyone would keep a ledger of hangings. It was like they thought this was an honorable thing worth recording. Most of the hangings took place before 1900 and several happened in the ten years after Josiah's hanging. It was as if a trend was started with Josiah's public execution. Most of those were listed as runaways, thieves, or some other trumped-up charge. Obviously these individuals were never brought to a court of law.

It was the final two names that jumped out at me. The second to the last was a girl: *Ruth Charles, 18 years old, 1950, crimes against nature/Klan.* The last entry: *Caleb Anderson, 17 years old, 1952, suicide.* Joseph noticed that my finger rested between those two names.

"The final two victims of the tree were young," Joseph said.

"Can you tell me anything about them?" I asked.

"Sure can," Joseph said. "The hanging ended where it started, with the Anderson family." He sighed.

"Even Ruth?" I asked.

"Yes, even Ruth. She was a beauty, and smart. That girl was the whole package. Even the white boys would watch her as she walked by; full of confidence that one was," Joseph said in a matter-of-fact tone.

"How could anyone like that do something that would get her hanged?" I asked.

"Ruth was one of those girls that every young man desired; but she had dreams of going to college and making something of herself, so she wanted nothing to do with any boys. She knew her dreams took money and lots of it. Ruth worked summers for the Anderson family; she hated it, but it was good money: odd jobs at the beginning and then in the house cooking and cleaning. It was there she meet a very young, very dashing, and very charismatic Clive Anderson IV," Joseph said.

"You mean the same Clive that's Maggie May's father in-law?"

Joseph nodded, saying, "One and the same, except back then, he hadn't hardened yet, like he is today. Back then, Clive was just a mischievous, rebellious teenager looking to have fun. He had his daddy's money and his mother's good looks and charm."

"So he was a *player*, or at least that's what the kids would call him nowadays," I said with a smile.

Joseph returned the smile and said, "I have no idea what that is, but Clive had no trouble attracting the ladies. Like I said, Ruth was a beauty, and even Clive couldn't ignore her allure. Ruth totally ignored Clive, as if he didn't exist, at first. Of course, this only intrigued Clive more. The thrill of the danger that existed for the two teenagers became too much of a temptation. Clive was sneaking candy and flowers to Ruth when no one was looking, walking Ruth home. It wasn't long before the two of them were head over heels in love."

"Clive in love with a black girl?! How did his parents take the news?" I asked.

"Therein lies the problem, you see. They both knew that their parents would kill them if they knew about the affair. A black-white romance in the South was forbidden back then. Throw in the fact that Clive was an Anderson, and it was a recipe for disaster. The knowledge of all this just seemed to fuel the relationship; it was like pouring gas on a flame. They were just crazy teenagers," Joseph said, shaking his head.

It was hard for me to believe a descendent of the Colonel could be in love with a black girl. The thought of it just made me smile. *I hope he saw it all,* I thought. The teenage romance sounded so sweet that I hated to find out what happened next. I just assumed they were caught and Clive's father hanged Ruth. "So what happened?"

Joseph continued, "Well...Ruth got pregnant—"

I gasped. "Oh no!"

"Clive and Ruth were determined to keep the baby, move away, and live happily ever after. Unfortunately, the doctor who was seeing Ruth for her pregnancy found out who the father was—"

I gasped again. "He didn't! Tell me he didn't rat them out?!"

"Yes, the doctor was an old friend of Clive III and a member of the local chapter of the Klan," Joseph said. "How could he? Besides that, if he was a member of the Klan, why did he treat black people?"

"Black people's money spent the same as white people's money; besides, he was trying to hide his affiliation with the Klan," Joseph said.

"On the eve of Clive and Ruth's planned escape, Clive III confronted his son with his newly acquired knowledge. The boy told his father he was in love with Ruth, and nothing was going to keep him from being with her. Of course, his father said absolutely not while he was alive, and they got into a horrible fight. His father knocked him out and tied him up so he couldn't leave. At the same time, the Klan was paying a visit to Ruth. They took Ruth as she was walking home by herself from a friend's house. The initial intent had been to beat her and scare her into ending the relationship, but things got out of hand; some of the Klansmen didn't appreciate the strength and opposition that Ruth displayed. To teach her—and all like her—a lesson, they hanged her." Joseph sighed.

My heart fell to my stomach. "No one was prosecuted?" I asked naïvely. Joseph just shook his head. I needed to know more. "What happened to Clive IV?"

"He was devastated. Clive fell into a deep depression and then just turned plain mean, and he hated all black people from then on," Joseph said.

"Wow...why hate black people?" I asked.

"It was his father who made that happen. His father convinced him that he'd been put under some kind of voodoo spell, some kind of witchcraft stuff that only black people practice. He made Ruth out to be a devil. In Clive's weakened mental state and need for resolution, he bought into it the whole story rather than facing the truth."

I needed to move on, so I asked, "How was Caleb related to Clive Anderson?"

"He was another son of Clive III, Clive IV's younger brother," Joseph said.

"Was his death a suicide, or is that just what they said happened?"

"No, his death was a suicide," Joseph said matter-of-factly. "You see, Caleb, he was a little different. He was what some people would refer to as soft, if you know what I mean," Joseph said, looking at me as he raised his eyebrows.

"Oh, so he was gay. I bet that went over well in the Anderson household," I said sarcastically.

"Back then, no one talked about it, and Caleb did his best to keep his actions in check, but his father and others knew he was different. This infuriated Clive III. Caleb was an embarrassment to him and the family, and Clive III did everything in his power to try to toughen Caleb up, as he put it. Clive's wife tried to shelter Caleb from his father's rampages, which made it worse on Caleb's other brother Arnold."

"Worse on Arnold?" I said in a questioning tone.

"Yes, Clive was bound and determined not to have another one go bad on him, as he put it, so he took all his anger out on Arnold. Clive's thinking was that if he was hard on Arnold, it would make him tough."

"Well, I've seen for myself how that worked," I said.

"Yes, all it did was break poor Arnold's spirit, especially after Caleb's death," Joseph said.

"Mary, Caleb's mother, took Caleb everywhere with her; she feared for his safety if she left him home with his father. It was on their many shopping trips that Caleb met an older man, a shoe salesman from Biloxi. Caleb took a shine to him and the man to Caleb. The man started visiting Larksburg more often and coming to the Anderson's to see if they needed to order any new shoes. It was on one of those visits that Clive III found Caleb and the man in the throes of passion in the barn," Joseph said, pausing for a moment.

"I bet Clive III went berserk!" I said.

"That's putting it mildly. Clive III beat the man unrecognizable, and when he was finished, he stood above Caleb, pointed a finger at him, and announced that Caleb was dead to him, that he was an abomination in his eyes and the eyes of the Lord.

"Having been found out, Caleb was shattered and terrified. He stared at the lifeless body of his partner and wept. Then anger filled Caleb's body; he grabbed a rope and a horse from the barn and headed toward town. Caleb made a sign that said *I am an abomination to my father* and pinned it to his chest. He threw the rope over the branch of the tree, created a noose, and tied the rope off at the base. He mounted his horse, slipped the noose around his neck with tears streaming down his face, and spurred his horse hard. With the snap of that rope, the hanging tree claimed its last victim."

Joseph and I sat in silence until we were interrupted by a familiar voice over the intercom. The librarian was reminding everyone that the library would be closing soon. I looked at Joseph, smiled, and thanked him for the information.

Joseph just nodded and said, "I hope it helps."

I didn't know how today's information was going to help, but I had a very strong feeling about the last two names on the list. I was going to trust that somehow the connections would all make sense. I thanked Joseph again and headed out.

I decided to go by the grocery store on my way home to pick up a few items. I was secretly hoping to see Josephine again. Unfortunately, when I arrived at the store, Josephine was nowhere to be found, and her grandson just glared at me as I shopped. I grabbed the items and headed home. I was looking forward to relaxing and listening to the radio.

CHAPTER 9

CALEB AND RUTH

Mornings were becoming routine now: coffee, radio, breakfast, and staring out my window at the tree. I replayed Josiah's horrible death and imagined the last hours of Ruth's and Caleb's lives, wondering why they seemed so tied together for me. The three of them didn't know each other; the only commonality was the Anderson family. Ruth's and Caleb's spirits were still at the tree, but why? I needed to go back. This time I wasn't going to be frightened away by Josiah's intimidation tactics. I didn't fear him; I knew I was stronger and more resilient. I knew Josiah was trying to scare me away to prove a point—that he was not worthy of salvation.

I had plenty of experience with this as a teacher. I had so many kids who'd come from abusive, challenging homes where they felt no one cared. They were very careful of trusting people and scared of success. They'd never experienced achievement themselves; it was always other people flourishing. These kids would sabotage their futures because of their internal fears of having something more in life—neither they nor anyone they knew had success. They would challenge authority, do anything and everything to try to make teachers mad or think they were beyond help. They wanted to prove to themselves that they couldn't be successful; personal success terrified them. In the end it was those who could overcome their fear who went on and those who could not that were doomed to repeat the past. It was our job as teachers to push them to see their own light to a future beyond their circumstance.

They wanted to prove they didn't deserve to be loved, by doing everything to chase people away before they had a chance to abandon them. They'd been abandoned and forgotten so much in their lives that the pain became too much to handle, so it was easy to justify it in their actions before it happened in reality. Only when you had battled through everything they could throw and were still standing there, telling them they could do it, did they trust you. Then the same kid would have a bad day or week, and it started all over again.

After my first encounter with Josiah, I knew I was going to have to take a lot more aggravation before I would gain his trust. I knew how persistent I was and how much I truly cared about Josiah. I finished the rest of my coffee and made a visit to the tree. As I approached the meadow, I felt a slight choking effect, but with every step I took, my breathing became easier, and my confidence level rose. The closer I got to the tree, the darker the sky seemed, and the air stood still. I had a feeling it was another attempt by Josiah to scare me.

I shouted out, "Caleb...Ruth!"

Josiah then popped out from behind the tree quickly. "Youse back again?" he asked angrily.

"Yes, I am, Josiah, but I'm not here to talk to you this time. I'm here to speak with Caleb and Ruth." I looked around, in an attempt to almost ignore Josiah. I figured it was time for a little tough love. I wanted him to know I wasn't scared, and I was in charge of the moment.

"What youse want wit 'em?" Josiah said, pacing around me in an intimidating manner.

"I just want to talk to them, since you don't seem interested in conversation."

Josiah laughed and pointed. I looked down, and my hair was again on the ground at my feet.

I calmly walked over to Josiah and said, "Your tricks will no longer frighten me; I see you, and any attempt you make to try to make me think you're unworthy of love won't work. Be gone so I may speak to Ruth and Caleb."

Josiah looked shocked, but he disappeared quickly.

The moment Josiah disappeared, two people materialized from behind the tree.

"Ruth? Caleb?"

They both nodded their heads yes. They were so young—they could have been my students. Ruth was everything Joseph said she was. She was stunning—tall and slender with high cheekbones and beautiful eyes. Caleb was small in stature, a very unassuming character, the stereotypical shy next-door-neighbor kind of kid. They both gazed at me in amazement.

"No one's ever talked to Josiah like that," Ruth said.

"Well, I'm going to be speaking to him like that a lot more if he doesn't lose the hostility," I said and then smiled.

They looked at each other, seemingly searching for some kind of answer to my presence and attitude.

"I've been looking forward to meeting the two of you. Why don't we sit down," I said, trying to let them know I was a friend.

"Us…why us?" Ruth said.

"I want to know your story. I want to help you be with your people," I stated.

"We don't got no people...none that'd want to see us again," Ruth said angrily.

"What makes you think that?" I asked.

"Josiah said when you do wrong by your people on Earth, you'd be tortured if you move on," Caleb said, hanging his head.

"We'd be condemned to hell," Ruth added.

"What?! Do you really believe your people and God are up there waiting for you with a baseball bat in hand?" I said, shaking my head.

I realized my comment was not well received. The skies turned darker, and the wind started to swirl. Ruth stood up and looked down on me with intense anger.

"You don't know! You don't know noth'n'!" Ruth shouted. "You don't know what we been through. You don't know what it's like to see hurt and disappointment in your parents' eyes and know you the one that put it there! I never saw my Daddy cry till the day I told him I was pregnant with a white man's baby. When they hanged me, I was almost glad so's I didn't have to spend the rest of my life knowing how I'd disappointed my parents," Ruth said, fuming.

"So you'd rather spend an eternity holding on to regret?" I asked. This comment earned me a very stern look from Ruth.

"It's better here than on the other side," Ruth said, a fiery tone in her voice.

"How do you know for sure?" I asked.

"'Cause Josiah told us, and he's been here a long time; he's done right by us. He said they'd never let us move on," Ruth said.

"Who are they?" I asked.

Quick eye contact happened between Ruth and Caleb.

"None o' yer business who they are," Ruth retorted.

I glanced at Caleb, who was stoic. "So how do you feel, Caleb?"

"It's no secret what happens to people like me," Caleb said.

"People like you? You mean, homosexuals?" I asked.

Caleb just nodded his head.

"Ruth and Josiah've been kind and took me in. I don't think it would be like that for me anywhere else," Caleb said sorrowfully.

I took a slow, deep breath and contemplated my words very carefully; I didn't want to challenge Ruth and Caleb, yet it was hard for me to understand their feelings.

"Caleb…I admire your loyalty to Josiah, and I don't want to make either of you feel like I'm trying to diminish your feelings—"

"Well don't then!" Ruth snapped at me.

I envisioned wrapping my arms around them both and holding them, because I knew I didn't have the right words to take their pain away. I looked at them both and could feel their fear of what I might say next. I knew I needed to slow down a bit and not push things.

"Tell you what, let's back up a bit and just get to know a little about each other first."

I told Ruth and Caleb about growing up on a farm, getting married to Joel, having three kids, and about Joel's death. They both listened without interruption, except I could tell there was some discontent brewing.

Ruth spoke first. "Your life seems like some story book or something. How's someone like you gonna understand people like us. We'd be outcasts; we'd be hated. Do you have any idea what it's like to be stared at, spit at, called names because o' the color o' your skin? White people stare at you like you're dirty. When you go in the store, they don't want you touching anything because they think you pack diseases like some rodent," Ruth said, rage in her voice.

"I was smart, real smart, but did anyone care about that? No! I was just another worthless piece of black trash to them," Ruth said, and then she took a swing with a closed fist into the empty air. "I knew I could go places if I just got a chance, but I knew the white people, they'd always want to win; they'd never want to give you a chance. My parents always lived in fear of the white people. They'd tell me, 'Now, Ruth, don't be doing anything to make the white people look at you; don't give 'em no cause.' To hell with that. I was just as good as any white person, and they knew it too. Even Clive said so..." Ruth stopped and played with a small gold band on her finger.

"So Clive was supportive of you?" I asked.

"Not at first, he acted like all the rest when he was with his friends. But, I could tell he was different; when his pappy wasn't around, he'd always be doing stuff for me, bringing me wild flowers and such. I didn't trust him, so I'd pretend that I couldn't care less if he brought me anything. Then one day he packed a picnic lunch, and he put me on his horse and took me to the lake. I was terrified we'd be caught, or someone would see and tell our parents. He was the perfect gentleman, and we talked about our dreams. He told me I was unlike any girl he'd ever met, white or black. I was a proud girl, and I took noth'n' from no one. Clive said I was the most courageous person he ever met." Ruth was smiling the whole time she told her story of Clive and their romance.

"I think we both started to enjoy the danger; the bigger the risks we took, the more powerful we felt. I remember riding horses in the pasture at midnight after we'd both sneaked out to meet. We were laughing as the horses galloped along. I remember feeling free, free from everything: my parents, and Clive's parents, but mainly free from my pain. It was that night that Clive and I made love, and it was the first time in my life I didn't feel black. As Clive held me in his arms and caressed my body, I felt human for the first time," Ruth said, her voice slowly drifting to a soft tone.

When Ruth finished her story, I felt such heaviness in my whole body. How could we have taken this beautiful, smart young woman and made her feel that the color of her skin was not tied to a human race but to a lifelong proclamation of social torture. I wanted to cry; maybe I wasn't the person for this job. I looked at Ruth with tears in my eyes and said the only thing I felt like I could say, "I'm so sorry for what you went through."

An apology was the only thing I had to offer; I felt so inadequate.

Ruth looked at me as if shocked by my statement and simply said, "Thank you." She sat down, her demeanor calmer, and smiled at me.

Caleb still sat stoically quiet, not commenting the whole time Ruth spoke.

"Caleb, did you know of your brother's relationship with Ruth?"

Caleb shook his head no.

"Caleb was always in his room or with his mother. I don't even remember seeing him much," Ruth said.

Caleb raised his head and said, "I did know he was seeing someone because he was always sneaking out. I always wanted to talk to him, but he never wanted to have much to do with me. No one ever wanted much to do with me. I wasn't like Ruth. People didn't spit at me or call me names. At least, not to my face—I think they were scared of my dad. People would just whisper and look at me and smile and laugh. I was the butt of a lot of jokes in this county. I started to realize there was something wrong with me when I was little. I loved to dress in my mother's clothes. My father never liked the way I talked with my hands or the way I walked or basically anything I did. He always told me to stop acting like a fruit, how I was such an embarrassment. He constantly blamed my mother for my affliction," Caleb said, rolling his eyes.

Affliction—this poor kid thought he was a disease, with no known cure, I thought.

On the bright side, I felt like I had turned on a water facet with Caleb: maybe this was the first time he felt free to talk about his situation. Caleb showed no signs of slowing down—he seemed determined to get his story out.

"My mother always felt sorry for me and acted like she didn't quite know what to do. I think she thought by taking me to Jackson and Biloxi with her all the time, it would keep me away from my father and out of public view, both of which were key to my survival.

"Unfortunately, my mother had extremely low self-esteem and believed my father when he said it was all her fault. One time when we were in Jackson, she took me to a doctor who said they could try electric shock therapy on me. The doctor said they'd had real good results with the treatment. I begged my mother not to do it; I told her I would change. The doctor told her I was mentally ill and probably belonged in an institution. I remember her telling the doctor she would talk it over with her husband. It was during the visit that I heard the term *homosexual tendencies* for the first time. The doctor had written down that *the patient exhibited extreme homosexual tendencies*." Caleb paused, gripped his hands tightly together, and let out a loud growl of frustration before continuing.

"No one seemed to realize how badly I wanted to be normal. I wanted to be like my brothers and father. Mainly how badly I wanted to be loved or touched by anyone. My mother, who had always been a very demonstrative person, no longer felt like she could touch me. My father had told her she had babied me too much, hugged and coddled me as a child, and that's why I didn't become a man. I remember longing for any kind of affection. My mother would forget sometimes and put her hand on my shoulder—only to quickly remove it and back away. I even started to like it when my father would push me into a wall because I was in his way and he needed to get by. Any kind of human contact, even violent interaction, felt good. It was as if my body just yearned for it." Caleb looked up, glancing at Ruth and me.

I couldn't help but notice, as I watched Caleb speak, how he would twist and contort his body as if he was still feeling every emotional blow. He was so incredibly articulate and intelligent. *What a waste!* I thought. *This kid could have been something great; both Ruth and Caleb could have been great.*

Caleb took a long, slow breath before he continued. "My mother was obsessed with shoes; she must have owned a million pairs. I guess not just shoes, but clothes in general. I think she was always trying to do anything to make my father notice her. The woman never ate; she was as thin as a blade of grass."

Ruth interrupted, saying, "I can attest to that. I used to work in the Anderson kitchen and she never ate, no matter what we put in front of her."

"I often thought she might have longed for attention as much as I did. I wondered if she was having affairs with the countless dressmakers, shoe salesmen, and hairdressers she saw. However, most of them were from the same cloth as me," Caleb said with a smile.

It was the first time I'd seen him smile. It seemed the more he told his story, the more pressure and pain released from him.

"In fact, it was the encounters with those men when I learned more about myself and felt I wasn't alone. One time, I heard a hairdresser refer to me as Mary's little queer son. It was the first time I heard *queer* instead of *homosexual.* The men were always pleasant to me; I think they knew what I was going through. They all were appropriate, never trying anything sexual with me. I started looking forward to going with my mom on her shopping sprees in hopes we would encounter homosexual men. I wanted to see how they acted and were treated by adults. None of them told anyone they were homosexual of course, but I guess we all belonged to a secret club and could just tell by a certain look," Caleb said, again with a smile and a glance at Ruth and me.

"It wasn't until I was sixteen and I met Harold, a shoe salesman, that I started to have strong sexual feelings for another man. My mother said no one could fit her feet like Harold. Of course, Harold had a trick—he rubbed off the 11 1/2 shoe size that my mother actually wore and replaced it with a 5 1/2. Lord, that woman had some big feet for such a small body," Caleb said. Ruth and I both chuckled.

"Harold was twenty-one, tall and slender, and always dressed like he worked in a bank. He told me he was saving up to go to business school. From the first time I saw him, I knew he was special. It wasn't long before he was delivering shoes to my mom at the house, and we would sneak off together. Harold was the only person who ever treated me with respect. The two of us had big plans; Harold was going to get his business degree, and we were going to move to Europe and own a vineyard. We spent hours planning every part—

from when he would graduate and how much money we would have to save. It was those dreams that would take us away from our reality." Caleb stopped and was wringing his hands. He asked, "Do you think he ever forgave me?"

"Forgave you for what?" I asked.

"For meeting him…it seems I never brought anyone I ever met anything but pain. Had he never meet me, he could have had the life he deserved," Caleb said.

"It sounds to me like you deserved and needed each other. You should lay the blame and pain at the feet of the person who created it," I stated.

Caleb looked at me and said, "My father."

"Yes, your father," I said.

"You know…I would've done anything to get my father to love me." Tears formed in Caleb's eyes.

"I know, Caleb. The lack of love from him isn't the fault of anything you did or didn't do. The fault lies within him and his fears and inability to overcome those fears. The evil of your father was guided by his father's hand and his father before him. Your father didn't have the strength of character you have, Caleb," I said.

Caleb gazed at me in disbelief.

Ruth cleared her throat. "You know, my Clive, he saw all that…you know all that stuff you said about his father and his father before him. He always told me that he was going to be different than them. He wasn't going to be cruel. Clive would always read me poems—he loved Edgar Allan Poe. His favorite was a poem entitled 'A Dream Within a Dream.' He had it memorized and would recite it to me all the time. Clive always knew he was meant to be different, to be better, but evil got him, didn't it?" Ruth looked at me for the answer.

"I don't know for sure, Ruth" I said.

"Caleb said he got real sad after my death and then turned mean, just like his pappy," Ruth said with disgust while tears welled in her eyes. "I should have known he was weak." Anger shook her words.

Caleb looked at Ruth and said, "I'm not sure it was weakness."

"What do you mean?" Ruth asked.

"I think it was hopelessness. I know what it looks like because I've felt it forever. I believe you have too, Ruth," Caleb said sheepishly.

"Hopelessness! Clive had it all! He could have followed his dreams! He could have stood up to your father! What did he have to be hopeless about?" Ruth said.

"His hope lived in what the two of you had together. When you died, so did he. It was as if any desire to get out and away disappeared. He became just another Clive Anderson—almost like he was possessed by all the Clives that came before him," Caleb said in a solemn tone.

Ruth stood up and stared at the ground. I waited anxiously for a response, but she spoke not a word.

Ruth slowly raised her head and said, "I'm done talking." Then she turned swiftly and disappeared.

Caleb looked at me and said, "I think I should go too." As Caleb turned to leave, he stopped, smiled, and said, "Thank you."

Before I could respond, he was gone.

The weight of profound sadness hung in the air. I sat at the base of the tree, resting my back against the trunk. Tears streamed down my face as I sobbed into my knees. I felt every emotion they felt as their stories unfolded. The inhumanity of it all was overpowering. I had to remind myself I was talking to spirits and not living, breathing human beings.

It didn't seem fair to compare anything I had gone through in my life with their struggles, almost embarrassing to even think of myself ever in their category of pain. The feeling of being an outcast by society because of no fault of your own goes beyond cruel.

I couldn't help remembering my junior year in high school when I had a run in with the mean-girl group at school. Every high school has a group of popular girls that everyone wants to be a part of but secretly hates. There are always at least a couple of girls in the group who are somewhat civilized and nice—when they're by themselves. I had known one of the nice girls since kindergarten.

Susan Price was my neighbor, and we'd grown up together, riding horses back and forth between our farms, showing cattle together at the county fair. We shared all our secrets; she was my best friend—up until our freshmen year in high school. I was into sports, and Susan was a cheerleader. We went in different directions but remained friends, just not as close. As we got older, Susan's friends became crueler as they moved up the social ladder of high school. In our junior year, I made the mistake of asking Susan a question while she was with her friends. I hadn't realized the offense I'd committed. Those girls declared me enemy number one. Their goal was to make my last year and a half of high school a living hell. It got so bad that people were even afraid to talk to me. The girls bullied me in every way they could—shoving me in the halls, spilling things on me at lunch, mocking me every chance they got. I was sick every morning before school—but I went, determined not to let them win. After graduating and going to college, I met Joel and Claire, and life was better.

Ruth and Caleb had no graduation. Ruth remained in a world of hate based on the color of her skin—a world in which her obstacles seemed like mountains, not hills. Caleb lived in a world where his true self was viewed as an illness, in a world where loving the person of your choice was considered an abomination. Both were caged, not for crimes, but for who they were. None of their experiences could even compare with my minor trials. I felt guilty for even trying to make the comparison. However it seems the mind goes to painful sources of reference when hearing the pain of others.

I walked across a stage, received a piece of paper, and was able to escape my world of torment. Ruth was always going to be black, Caleb always gay. Even in death, they're still tormented by life. I knew there was something better for them; I just needed to figure out how to get them to their graduation day.

As I contemplated how to help them while I approached the post office, I saw Maggie May standing at the corner waiting for me. She greeted me with her bubbly personality, but this time she had a somewhat-worried look on her face.

"You know people are really starting to talk about you spending so much time at the tree and researching at the library. People are starting to think you're touched in the head. Arnold said the other day you came running from the tree because you got stung by a bunch of bees. You don't look like you've been stung," Maggie said.

"Stung by bees? What? Oh…I get it now. No, I wasn't stung by bees, and I'm not touched in the head," I said sarcastically.

"Well, good, because I got you invited to the Anderson family picnic tomorrow out on the plantation. I kept telling them that you're not crazy, just eccentric," Maggie said, smiling. "So how're things going?"

"Great," I said, sounding like I was talking about work. "Things are moving right along."

"Will you tell me about it?" Maggie asked.

"Yes, of course I will. I have a lot of questions to ask you too," I said.

"Great! We can talk about it on our drive out to the plantation tomorrow. I'll pick you up at 11:30, okay?"

"Sounds good. Should I bring something?" I asked.

Maggie paused and thought for a moment. "Watermelon, that family loves watermelon."

"Okay, see you tomorrow," I said.

Well, I guess I'm off to the store to get watermelon, I thought, smiling to myself.

CHAPTER 10

THE PLANTATION

It was a beautiful Saturday morning; I nearly bounded out of bed. I was excited to go to the Anderson plantation—not really sure why I was so excited. These weren't exactly the kind of people I wanted to befriend, but I was hoping for answers. I prepared my coffee and sat at my table staring at the tree, thinking of Caleb and Ruth. Josiah was full of hostility, hate, and guilt, and maybe that played a role in why he hadn't moved on, but why Caleb and Ruth? They seemed so sweet and innocent: two beautiful souls taken before their time. But maybe that was just the mom voice in me. Everything that happened to them seemed so unfair and cruel. Not that what happened to Josiah wasn't on the same level. Maybe I was unhappy with Josiah because of his attitude toward me.

Right then, a little voice inside my head said, *Let...it...go.*

I showered, dressed, and awaited Maggie May's arrival. As I waited, I thought about meeting Hattie Anderson for the first time. I had heard so much about her from around town, and I was a little nervous.

Maggie's knock at the door brought me out of my daydream.

"Hey, Maggie."

Maggie looked me up and down. "Is that what you're wearing?" She grimaced but then quickly caught herself. "Oh, I'm so sorry, I didn't—"

"You said picnic!" I said, looking down at my Denver Broncos t-shirt, shorts, and flip-flops.

Maggie, on the other hand, had on a beautiful short-sleeved flowered dress, conservative pumps, and her hair was tied back in a bun.

"*Ugh!*" I exclaimed.

I went to my makeshift closet and grabbed a lavender flowered sundress. I held it up. "Will this work?"

Maggie giggled and nodded her head yes. I ran to the bathroom, changed, and grabbed a pair of dress sandals from my suitcase. I put on some stud earrings and a cross necklace the kids had gotten me last Christmas.

"Okay, is this conservative enough?" I said sarcastically.

Maggie again giggled. "Yes."

"I'm assuming we won't be playing cornhole or volleyball at this picnic."

"Cornhole, what's cornhole?"

"Seriously?"

I started to explain the game, but Maggie interrupted me.

"No games at these picnics, at least for the women. The men play horseshoes or cards, and the kids run around or ride horses or ATVs," Maggie said.

"So what do the women do?" I asked.

"Well…we talk." She threw me a sideways glance.

"Talk…we talk? About what?" I asked.

"I'm guessing, but I think today we'll talk about…you." Maggie burst into laughter.

"You little shit," I said with a sly grin.

I jumped into Maggie's minivan with my watermelon and looked around, expecting to see her husband and kids inside.

"What, no hubby and kids?" I asked.

"They're already there. They went out early to do some hunting with Papa Clive."

"Papa Clive...makes him sound like a kind, old grandpa," I said facetiously.

Maggie rolled her eyes. "Oh, by the way, Gary's parents can't stand it if anyone calls him Gary in their presence. So it's either Clive or his nickname C. A.," Maggie said as she bobbed her head back and forth, mocking their ridiculous demands.

"Got it," I said. "Any other little Anderson clan nuances I should know about?"

"It would take me days to go through them all; you're just going to have to be quick on your feet, and listen as much as possible when you're not being grilled, which I suspect will be the majority of the time," Maggie said with a sigh.

"So a little bob and weave mixed with a little rope-a-dope defense," I said, grinning.

"Rope a what? Bob and weave? What are you talking about?" Maggie shook her head.

"I guess you're not a boxing fan..." I said, chuckling.

Maggie started the car, still looking a little puzzled. As we made our way down Main Street and out of town, Maggie fired questions about the day before. I started with clearing up the bee story. First Maggie gasped, and then she laughed at the thought of everyone thinking it was because I'd been attacked by bees. However, when I started to talk about Ruth and Caleb, Maggie had a questioning look on her face. I remembered that look of disbelief from Joel when I told him about odd occurrences. I stopped talking, not quite knowing how to proceed.

We had only traveled about five miles when I saw a huge iron archway with large letters spelling out ANDERSON.

"This must be our turn," I said, breaking the silence with an awkwardly sarcastic tone.

Maggie went underneath the archway and onto Anderson Lane, not saying a word. I was feeling increasingly uncomfortable.

Maggie pulled the car off to the side of the road and placed it in park. She turned to look at me. "I want to believe you...I do. But it's getting weirder and weirder," Maggie said, stopping to clear her throat as if her next words were stuck. "I've always known and even experienced the mysterious things in this place and the stifling sense of...of fear, anger, hatred, depression. I don't know really what to call it. It's like a heaviness that's always there; sometimes it feels like it's hard to breath. But you're making all this *real*...a little too real—even for me," Maggie said, lifting her eyes from the floorboard to finally meet my gaze.

"Would you rather I not tell you?" I asked.

There was a short pause—I could see Maggie searching for her answer. Finally she blurted out, "*No!* I want to know." She sounded determined, but there was another short pause. "I'm all in—whatever you need from me; I want this to end for the sake of my children," Maggie said, a little quiver in her voice. She gazed hard into my eyes. "I believe you. I do. It's just hard to...do you know what I mean?"

"I know. Sometimes it's hard for me to believe it too. I just feel in my heart and soul that I'm meant to be here," I said.

"I think you are too."

With that, Maggie put the car in drive and we continued down the lane. The closer we came to the house, the harder my heart started to pound; my palms started to sweat. A strong feeling of dread was starting to come over me.

"Are you okay? You look white as a sheet," Maggie said.

"Yes, just a little anxious."

"Well, you better hold on tight because it only gets worse from here," Maggie said with her sly little chuckle that I was becoming accustomed to.

As I exited the car, I realized I'd been here before. My knees started to shake as I saw the whipping posts where Josiah had been beaten that night. My eyes moved slowly around the grounds. The house looked almost exactly the same: huge wraparound porch with majestic columns in front to frame an entry that looked like something out of *Gone with the Wind*. I glanced to where the slave quarters had been that night and there were still two buildings standing. I gasped.

Maggie May came around the car and saw me staring at the two remaining cabins.

"Can you believe they kept that crap around? It's a disgrace and an embarrassment if you ask me," Maggie said, a look of disgust on her face.

"Yes," was all I could say—I was still in shock.

"And to save these whipping posts—*ugh!* Papa Clive would always threaten to tie my boys up and give 'em a whippin' if they acted up! Made me sick," Maggie said, shaking her head.

As I finished looking around, everything else seemed relatively new and modern but with typical southern charm. It was what Maggie said it would be: I saw a game of horseshoes going on, boys riding ATVs, and some girls riding horses in an arena. Then a tall, well-built dark-haired man appeared and gave Maggie a peck on the lips.

"Hi, honey," Maggie said.

The man put his arm around Maggie and smiled at me.

"This is my husband, Gary."

This brought an immediate response from Gary. "Shhh, Maggie, Daddy's right over there!" Gary said.

"Oh sorry, I mean C. A.," Maggie said with her patented giggle.

"Nice to meet you, C. A. Thank you so much for inviting me to the family plantation," I said, reaching out and shaking Gary's hand.

"You may not be so grateful by the time this is all done," Gary said, swaying his head.

I wasn't sure how to respond; it was a somewhat awkward moment. So I just said, "I'm sure everything will be fine." It sounded so lame as it came out of my mouth.

Gary looked at Maggie and said, "I just hope you know what you've gotten yourself into here."

"Oh come on, Gary. It'll be fun! You heard her. Everything'll be just fine," Maggie said as she grasped Gary's arm, leaning her head on his shoulder, smiling, and gazing into his eyes.

As we walked toward the house, I couldn't help but replay the night of Josiah's death. I could see his naked, shackled body chained to the posts. The onlookers only interested in a good show. The crack of the whip as it tore into Josiah's scarred body. I felt my stomach start to tighten and the warmth of tears in my eyes, but I was snapped out of my daydream by the appearance of one of Maggie May's children.

"Hi, Mom," he said as he ran to greet us at the front steps to the house. "Can you tell Matt to stop following me everywhere? He's always bugging me," the boy said, frustration in his voice.

"We'll talk about that later." Maggie glanced sternly at him, as if her son was embarrassing her. Gary also gave a disapproving look and elbowed the boy in the arm.

"James, I'd like you to meet Mrs. Sara O'Reilly from Colorado; she's a teacher who is visiting the South," Maggie said. "Sara, this is James, our oldest."

By this time, Gary and Maggie's other child had joined us and the conversation. "Why would anyone want to visit here?" the boy blurted out.

This statement brought an immediate response from his parents—Gary lightly slapped the back of the boy's head.

Maggie May grimaced and said, "Matthew!" Maggie looked over at me. "I'm sorry, Sara. This is our youngest, Matt."

Matthew looked at the ground and said, "Sorry, ma'am."

"That's okay, Matt. It's nice to meet you. I'm growing very fond of the South, but when I was a kid growing up in a small town, I couldn't understand why anyone would want to come visit our area either," I said.

This brought a small grin to Matthew's face. He put out his hand for me to shake as he started his own introduction.

"Hi, I'm Matthew Anderson. But all my friends call me Matt. I'm twelve years old, and I'm going to be in the seventh grade next year. This is my brother, James, but everyone calls him Jim or Jimbo. He's fourteen and going into ninth grade. That's why he thinks he's too good to hang around with the rest of us," Matt said.

This comment brought a strong response from his brother.

"Maybe if you weren't such an annoying little twerp, I'd want you around," Jim said.

A shoving match broke out between the two boys, and Gary grabbed them both by the arms and dragged them off for a talk.

"I'm so sorry for their behavior; those two have been fighting nonstop this summer, and it's driving us crazy," Maggie said, shaking her head.

"I have kids too; I know how they can be at that age," I said.

The two boys came back over and apologized. I smiled and thanked them for the apology. They headed back to hop on the ATVs.

I started following Maggie up the stairs but then remembered I had forgotten the watermelon in the car. "Oh, shoot. I need to grab the watermelon."

"I'll go get it," Gary said.

I was almost wishing I could go—I was starting to lose my nerve—when Ms. Emma Jean met us at the door.

"Well, hello, Maggie May. It's been too long since you've been to a gathering," Emma Jean said with a smirk, which was her attempt at a smile I suppose.

I could tell that she was just antagonizing Maggie.

"I believe I was here just a month ago, Aunt Emma Jean," Maggie said with a fake smile.

"Oh, I guess it just seems longer. Oh and look. You brought your new friend. Ms. O'Reilly, is it?"

Right then my game plan formed; I would kill them with kindness, fight fire with fire. "Well, yes it is. How kind of you to remember, and may I add, that dress is just stunning. You southern women could sure teach us western women a little about fashion," I said, smiling and reaching out my hand to greet Emma Jean.

Maggie May looked shocked, but Emma Jean ate it up.

"Well, I never want to say anything bad about anyone, but us southern women know how to be ladies," Emma Jean said, bringing her hand to her chest, fingers spread, turning her head, and looking down her nose.

"When you're right, you're right, Ms. Jenkins," I said, following Emma Jean into the house.

She stopped, turned, and said, "Call me Emma Jean."

Maggie grabbed my wrist and pulled me back and whispered, "Where the hell did that come from?"

"I just tapped into my internal Stepford wife," I said with a chuckle.

Maggie nodded her head and smiled. "Good, you're gonna need it."

As we entered the house, I was taken aback by the grandeur of the foyer. There was a sitting room to the left and an office to the right, beautiful hardwood floors throughout, a magnificent curved staircase with a mahogany railing. The windows in the office and sitting room were very large and unique, the top one arched and the center fixed, while the sides opened to the outside. They were immense, in both size and character. The drapes were dark-red velveteen with hand embroidery along the top, which matched tie backs at the sides. I felt like I had entered a castle. The furnishings all looked like pristine antiques, absolutely nothing out of place.

Emma Jean recognized how rapt I was with the house, and she took great pleasure in showing it off. She spoke of its history and the importance of the Anderson family and how…well, she didn't want to brag, but they were basically southern royalty.

As Emma Jean yammered on like only she could, all kinds of smartass responses flew through my head; I fought them off and stayed in character.

"Well, you should be proud, Ms. Jenkins. This is a beautiful house and your family has such an amazing history. You tell it with such an articulate passion," I said in a sweet, syrupy voice.

Maggie rolled her eyes at me as my stomach churned. She interrupted Emma Jean's lengthy monologue of the Anderson family history and financial distinction. "Aunt Emma Jean, do you think we should move to the parlor?" Maggie said.

Emma Jean did not appreciate the interruption but did concur and directed me to the hallway. As we entered the hallway, the air seemed to cool, and the lighting darkened. I could see it was lined with pictures. It was like a museum, a pictorial of the Anderson family history. I walked slowly, trying to absorb every photo, or in some cases hand-drawn pictures. I saw a picture of Caleb and an artist rendition of the Anderson's plantation in the 1800s—it was just as I'd seen it the night of Josiah's murder.

Pictures of slaves working in the fields… I felt the overwhelming sadness that seemed to jump out of every picture. The true agony these walls held was overpowering and the history of misery devastating. Although Emma Jean only expressed pride.

We entered the parlor, and it was even more impressive than the foyer. The same hickory hardwood floors ran throughout the house. The high majestic windows with the beautiful hand-embroidered red-velveteen curtains were present. There was a large fireplace surrounded by inlaid stone and a dark walnut mantel. A life-size painting of the Colonel was displayed above the mantel with an engraved gold plaque positioned below.

An enormous crystal chandelier hung from the center of the room, giving off flickers of light blue. The furniture was all fine hardwood with supple-leather cushions, except for the hand-carved high-back dining chairs, which had red-velveteen cushions that matched the drapes. The massive dining table was absolute elegance with a pure-white tablecloth and beautiful dark-blue table runner. Small bouquets of magnolias and red and yellow roses were perfectly situated every two feet in the center of the runner.

The place settings were hand-painted china with dazzling silver utensils and large crystal water glasses filled with ice water, lemon wedges on the rims. There were about ten women in the room, all meticulously dressed and engaged in conversations.

I spoke over my shoulder to Maggie, "This is a picnic?"

The words had just passed my lips when I noticed a stern-looking woman standing behind Maggie. I swallowed hard; I knew it had to be Hattie Anderson. She blew by me as if I didn't even exist. Upon her entrance, the room immediately became dead silent, and all eyes were on Hattie. She walked across the room and stood in front of the fireplace, turning to address her guests.

I tried to stay focused on Hattie, but I just couldn't— my eyes kept drifting upward to the painting of the Colonel. He was dressed in a military uniform: tall black boots, sword at his side, wispy gray hair, and coal black eyes. It was his eyes that drew me to the painting; it almost seemed like he was staring right at me. I could feel the hairs standing up on the back of my neck, and a shiver went down my spine.

Maggie May's elbow to my ribs brought me back—she could see I wasn't giving Hattie my full attention, which she knew would bring me the woman's wrath. I refocused as

Hattie was wrapping up her welcome speech sprinkled with recent Anderson family accomplishments, mainly grandchildren winning awards or doing well at sporting events. As Hattie finished, she still hadn't looked my way. I thought by this point she would be all over me.

I turned to Maggie and said, "So, do you think Hattie heard my picnic crack and is pissed?"

"No, she won't acknowledge you until she's been formally introduced," Maggie said, rolling her eyes.

"Who is she, the queen?" I said sarcastically.

Maggie and I made our way over to Hattie. As we approached the gaggle of women who had surrounded her like adoring fans, they stopped talking and made a small passageway for us. Hattie was dressed in a pastel peach dress, pearl necklace with matching earrings, and a beautiful gold diamond wedding band. Her hair was a graying blond, tied back tightly, which accentuated her high cheekbones and slender, pointed nose.

"Hello, Mother Anderson. I would like to introduce you to Sara O'Reilly from Colorado. We met years ago at a conference—"

"So you're the one staying above the post office I've heard so much about," Hattie interrupted, looking down her nose at me.

The glare of her eyes was almost chilling, and the guests spoke not a word as all eyes were laser focused on me.

I smiled and said, "Yes, I am. And may I say what a pleasure it is to finally meet you, Mrs. Anderson. I've heard so much about you and your wonderful family."

I was fighting every instinct I had, trying to stay in character. Hattie's facial expression never changed as she looked me up and down; the corners of her mouth turned down with one of the most pronounced frowns I had ever seen.

Slowly, Hattie reached out her hand, ever so reluctantly, to shake mine. I could tell it was going to be one of those handshakes I hated. The type when women shake with their thumb and two fingers, as if afraid they're going to catch something, their grip like a wet noodle. However, I reciprocated the weak handshake. I refrained from grabbing her hand fully and shaking it wildly, saying, "Well howdy, ma'am."

The room was still and silent, waiting for Hattie to speak.

"So what brings you to Larksburg?" Hattie asked.

I felt the eyes in the room burning a hole through me as they anticipated my response.

"I have a friend in Jackson and, of course, Maggie May here, and basically I've always wanted to experience the South," I said, holding my fake, pasted-on smile.

"So you wanted to experience the South...then why not travel the South? Why come to Larksburg and stay?" Hattie said in a disbelieving tone.

"When I came here, I just loved the small-town atmosphere," I said.

I could tell that Hattie wasn't buying any of this, and the tension in the room was increasing.

"So you wandered in here and just decided to stay for a spell. I hear you've taken an interest in our famous oak tree in town. In fact, I hear you spend a lot of time out there and in the library researching the tree. Some think you're a reporter; others think you're touched in the head. Said they've seen you talking to yourself and acting crazy. So which is it?" Hattie said in a stern, almost-frightening voice.

I cleared my throat, trying not to act intimidated. I'd dealt with a lot of Hattie's in my day, and they thrived on fear. I looked her square in the eye, stood up straight, and said, "I'm no reporter, just a history lover; in fact, I'm a high school history teacher. As far as being crazy…I guess I've been accused of worse." I held my posture and kept her gaze, not flinching.

Hattie huffed and glared at me with eyes that could melt steel. A loud bell rang outside, and I heard Maggie sigh and say, "Thank God, the dinner bell."

I turned to Maggie, confused, as Hattie walked away. "The dinner what?"

"They ring the bell to let everyone know the food is ready. The kids all eat outside and the adults inside. Hattie doesn't like to deal with insects when she eats, so we never have a true picnic," Maggie said, snickering a little.

The men joined us, and we were all seated at the table, Clive at the head of the table by the fireplace and Hattie seated to his right. I couldn't help but notice the uncanny resemblance Clive had to the Colonel. The only differences were the clothing and Gary's dad's hair was cut short and was very well kept.

The food was being brought in by servants who then stood with loaded trays off to the side of the table. I assumed they were awaiting direction.

I whispered to Maggie, "What are they waiting for?"

"Grace, silly. They're waiting for Clive to say grace," Maggie whispered back.

Of course, I thought, almost chuckling to myself.

Then Clive started the prayer. "Dear Lord, please bless this food we are about to eat and bless those who have joined us today."

Wow, that's probably one of the coldest prayers I've ever heard, I thought.

The whole time, Clive's face never left his plate. As soon as he finished, he motioned for the food to be served.

The food was wonderful: chicken breast with mashed potatoes and gravy, green beans, and dinner rolls. Everything tasted great, but the environment still held an uneasy feeling.

I turned to my right to greet the person next to me, since all my attention and conversation had been with Maggie, who was on my left. I was surprised to see a ruggedly hand-some man, probably around fifty, seated next to me. He smiled, and I felt my body tingle a little, something that hadn't happened since before Joel died.

His eyes were crystal blue; his smile was a little crooked on one side and was outlined by a mustache. He reminded me of the actor Sam Elliot, and when he spoke, his voice was a deep baritone, solidifying the resemblance.

"Hello, ma'am, I'm Shawn Anderson."

I was so physically taken by him that I stammered like a nervous high school girl. "Um...it's nice...to meet you too. I'm...Sara O'Reilly." I felt my face getting warm. Then I realized he didn't say it was nice to meet me. My face was red hot now. "I mean...I mean...umm..." I was so tongue-tied.

Shawn just laughed and said, "No worries. That happens to me all the time. Most of the time, I don't know if I'm comin' or goin'. Besides I'm sure comin' here and getting questioned by Hattie hasn't been exactly stress free."

Shawn certainly had a way of quickly diminishing my embarrassment and uneasiness.

"I've only been through round one with Mrs. Anderson. I'm sure she has a lot more in store for me after lunch," I said.

"Well, maybe I can help you out. After we finish eating, I'll volunteer to take you on a tour of the estate; that will get you out of here," Shawn said with a wink and a smile.

I smiled back. "I'd like that very much."

I looked back at Maggie, and she was smiling. She leaned over and whispered in my ear, "He's a hottie, and he's single."

"Not interested," I whispered back.

I had to admit, if only to myself, that I was definitely attracted to Shawn. Voices were racing violently in my head. I thought about how Joel hadn't even been dead a year, how I was betraying him, his memory, the only man I'd ever truly loved. I felt such guilt, and all I had done was say hello. Maybe I was as crazy as the townspeople thought. I did long for Joel's touch, the way he would gently caress my body and kiss my neck. *Okay. Okay. I need to stop thinking—before I have a* When Harry Met Sally *moment.*

Clive tapped his water glass and stood. "If you gentlemen are done with your meal, we can continue with our horseshoe tournament." He turned to his wife, bobbed his head, looked up, and said, "Ladies, if you will please excuse us."

I looked down at my plate and realized I'd only taken four or five bites. I shoveled in a couple more bites of mashed potatoes and called it good.

"Don't forget, we'll be having desert in an hour, Clive, your favorite—peach pie," Hattie said as Clive walked from the room, hardly acknowledging her, but with a wave of his hand and a nod of his head.

As the men left the room, I saw Emma Jean and Hattie making a beeline toward me.

Maggie turned and said "Hold on tight; here it comes."

Shawn stepped in front of me, almost blocking me from the dual incoming torpedoes of Hattie and Emma Jean, and said "Ms. Hattie, would you mind if I escorted our guest on a tour of the grounds? She seems quite interested in your plantation."

Hattie and Emma Jean looked at each other with a mixture of anger and disappointment; they had me in their crosshairs.

"Well, I guess that would be okay, but don't be gone too long," Hattie said curtly.

I felt like I had just gotten out of having to go to the principal's office.

Shawn, being the perfect southern gentlemen, said, "After you, ma'am," as he pointed the way with his outstretched arm, guiding me out of the parlor.

"Well, thank you very much," I said with a schoolgirl giggle.

"Would you like your tour on horseback, Jeep, or ATV?" Shawn asked as we walked out the front door. I said the Jeep would be fine since it would give us more opportunity to talk.

Shawn was very friendly and talkative; he explained that Clive and Hattie were his cousins, and he lived near Houston, but he came up a couple months a year to help out. He owned a ranch of his own and had two grown sons, both of whom lived in Texas and refused to visit the Andersons in Larksburg.

"I think they're the smart ones. I'm not even sure why I keep coming. Habit, I guess, or…maybe I think things might change," Shawn said.

"Change?"

"You've been here for a little while—I know you see it. It's as if when you come here, everything turns black and white."

I'd never heard it expressed that way, and I knew Shawn wasn't speaking of racial issues but of emotional culture. I had to ask anyway. "Black and white?"

"Yeah, it's as if all the beautiful colors of the world get sucked out and the environment is just gray here. People smile and laugh and such, but there's no soul to it," Shawn said as he looked off into the distance.

Wow! I thought. *This guy gets it. He's one of those rare people—beautiful inside and out—his wife is one lucky gal.* So again, I had to ask.

"Is your wife down in Houston?"

Shawn stopped the Jeep and stared at the steering wheel.

"She passed ten years ago...breast cancer, it took her fast. I don't really like to talk about it; I miss her so much," Shawn said, his voice thick with emotion.

"I understand," I said.

"I know you do." Shawn gave me a small smile.

"Small town," I said.

"Yep, small town, big gossip."

Our conversation about spouses ended, and we went on to less painful topics. He went into great detail about how the plantation used to grow mainly tobacco and cotton but currently had switched to soybeans, sweet potatoes, and cotton. They also had a large herd of cattle they pastured. Although Shawn's guided tour was interesting, I couldn't help but fixate on a hill that was about a half mile away. It seemed to be enclosed with a tall black-iron fence with a small shed in the middle.

"What's that on the hill?" I asked.

"Oh that...that's the Anderson family cemetery," Shawn said, groaning a bit.

"A cemetery? The family has its own cemetery...well that's interesting. Can we go see it?" I asked, probably sounding a little too excited.

"You want to see a cemetery? That place gives me the creeps, and in my opinion, that's where evil goes to die—or live, depending on how you look at it," Shawn said.

"Please, I'm interested in history. Is that where the first Clive Anderson is buried?"

"Yes, he is. Are you sure you want to go up there? We can't even get anyone to cut the grass or maintain the place because people are so scared," Shawn said.

"Are you scared?" I asked.

Shawn puffed up and said, "Of course not!"

As we drove closer to the cemetery, Shawn told me a story about three high school boys who came out on a dare from fellow classmates. The boys, he said, stole the head off the large granite statue of the Colonel and were on their way back to the high school to show it off when the car veered off the road. The car rolled, catching on fire, and the boys were unable to escape.

I cringed, thinking about the terrible death the boys had. Shawn paused for a moment, but then finished the story by telling me how the head of the statue was found totally intact with no damage other than that caused by the boys when they knocked it off its base.

"Hattie hired a guy to fix the statue…as soon as he finished the job, he died of a massive heart attack right outside the gates of the cemetery. Some people think of fear, others think the Colonel killed him out of spite." Shawn stopped, looked at me, and started to laugh after he made ghost sounds.

"Is any of that true?" I asked.

"Unfortunately all of it, but it happened twenty years ago, and no one has been up here since. I think it was just coincidence," Shawn said.

As we pulled up to the cemetery, I saw that the iron fortress was impressive, to say the least. The fence was made of wrought iron and had to be at least seven or eight feet tall. There were large four-by-four poles in the ground with two-inch black rods running the length; the rods were arrow capped. On both sides of the large gate were iron Confederate flags. We both stood about ten feet from the entry, just gazing at the size of the enclosure.

Shawn broke the silence. "Makes you wonder if they're trying to keep something out or something in," he said with a chuckle.

"No kidding, seems like a little overkill, pardon the pun," I said, and we both laughed.

As we walked closer, I saw the large granite statue of the Colonel; it was more like a monument. Several large trees granted shade, but the grounds were overrun with weeds. I could see what I assumed was a pump house in the back and several headstones. The closer we came to the gate, the harder my heart pounded and my chest tightened—just as it had when Claire and I entered the cemetery in Vicksburg. I felt stronger now than I did then; I was determined not to back down.

Shawn struggled with the gate. It was apparent it hadn't been opened in a long time and was quite rusted. He finally managed to get one side to open far enough for us to fit through. As Shawn stepped back and said, "After you, my lady," he stepped in a hole, twisting and going down hard. "Oh, my ankle!"

"Are you okay?" I asked, squatting down next to him.

"I twisted my ankle. I hope it's not broken," he said.

I was able to get his foot out of the hole and his boot off—he was in a lot of pain, and his ankle was swelling fast.

"We need to get you back to the house."

I helped him up and back to the Jeep. I put him in the passenger seat since there was no way he could drive. I shut the door, turning to walk around the Jeep. When I looked up at the gate of the cemetery, there stood the Colonel, laughing.

"I'll be back," I said to him, and the Colonel vanished.

When I jumped into the driver's seat, Shawn asked me what I'd said.

"Oh, nothing, just what a day."

Shawn hung his head. "I'm sorry. I just didn't see the hole."

"Oh, not you…this isn't your fault. That's not what I meant at all."

We drove in silence back to the house.

Ugh, my mouth, I thought.

CHAPTER 11

AWAKENING

I struggled to sleep after the day at the Anderson's. I tossed and turned, only sleeping for short periods at a time. I finally gave up around 5:00 a.m. and decided to get up and make myself some coffee. I turned on the radio and sipped my coffee, replaying the disastrous end, which played out once Shawn and I returned to the house.

You would have thought Shawn had been shot or something, the way people reacted. Everyone ran around, saying they would be the ones taking him to the hospital, as if taking him was some sort of honor. Hattie and Emma Jean glared at me, asking me what I had done to him.

What I had done to him?! I thought. *What, did they think I took him out back, threw him down, and jumped up and down on his ankle?*

I started to explain, but Shawn broke in abruptly and said, "We were down by the cattle, and I stepped in a prairie dog hole."

He quickly threw me a glance, and I knew I was supposed go along with his story. The chatter stopped, and everyone looked at me, awaiting my response. "Yes...he stepped in a hole and hurt his ankle." This seemed to satisfy everyone's curiosity as to how it happened, except Hattie. She continued to glare at me as if I were guilty of assaulting him.

Hattie slowly walked over to me. "When I saw you driving back, you weren't coming from the direction of the pasture."

Before she could say anything else, Shawn asked if I could get his cell phone from the Jeep. Hattie's eyes were still locked with mine when I said, "I must've gotten a little lost and turned around out there a few times trying to get Shawn back. Now if you'll excuse me, I need to get his phone."

I ran over to the Jeep to get the phone as Hattie and Emma Jean huddled in discussion. Maggie followed me.

"Gary and I are going to take Shawn to the hospital to get an x-ray. Take my keys. I think you should get out of here before the vultures pick you clean. I'll get my van back tomorrow," Maggie said, whispering so no one else could hear.

I grabbed her keys and turned to thank Clive and Hattie for their hospitality. I was stopped in my tracks by their steely demeanor.

"Thank you..." I said awkwardly.

I looked at Shawn and mouthed *I'm sorry* as I waved to him. No other guests exchanged pleasantries with me. In fact, I think they were glad to see me go.

The next morning, I struggled with the thought of Shawn not wanting anyone to know we were at the cemetery. A loud knock at the door startled me out of my thoughts. I opened the door and Maggie burst through. I could tell she was upset—her eyes were wide, and she was breathing heavily.

"What were you thinking?" Maggie asked, her hands on her hips.

"What are you talking about?" I said. Her demeanor confused me.

"I can't believe you asked Shawn to take you to the cemetery!"

"Well...I didn't know it was such a big deal or that it was off limits," I said somewhat sarcastically.

"Well it is!" Maggie huffed.

"Please sit down, Maggie. I'll get you a cup of coffee." She pulled out a chair and sat down. Her arms were crossed, and she was visibly angered.

"Look, Maggie, I didn't mean to cause you any problems, but I needed to see it—I needed to be there, and I'll be going back," I said insistently.

Maggie leapt to her feet. "Oh no you won't! Do you have any idea how much trouble you've caused me? Gary and I have been fighting ever since Shawn told us. This is the biggest fight we've ever had. He stormed out this morning without even giving me a ride here; I had to ask my neighbor," Maggie shouted, tears in her eyes.

"I'm sorry about the fight between you and Gary, but I'm not sorry about going there, and I'm not asking your permission to go back," I said, standing my ground.

Over the years, I'd learned that women say *I'm sorry* way too much when they haven't done anything wrong. I knew that Maggie's anger was about the fight with Gary and not about me. I felt bad they'd gotten in a fight, but I wasn't sorry for my actions. I had grown to appreciate Maggie and her friendship and didn't want to jeopardize our relationship. But I wasn't going to let anything stand in the way of me returning to the cemetery and confronting the Colonel.

Maggie's head rose and our eyes locked; tears were now streaming down her face. "I'm scared, Sara. I'm just scared," Maggie said as she dropped her head into her hands and began to sob.

I grabbed a box of Kleenex and sat them on the table near Maggie. She immediately grabbed one and blew her nose.

"Of what exactly? What are you scared of?" I was almost pleading for some sort of explanation that would make sense of all this.

"It's hard to explain. I'm not sure I really even know. I just have this overwhelming feeling of dread," Maggie said, shaking her head.

This wasn't the answer I was expecting. "Dread...why?"

"I think it's just the fear of not knowing what's coming next. I know things around here always seem in a dark cloud, or at least that's how I've always felt since coming here. I think people here try to be nice, but they always seem to be living in fear," Maggie said.

"Fear of what? The Andersons...the past...each other...what?" I wanted her to spell it out for me.

Maggie took a sip of her coffee, her eyes fixed on the rim of her cup. "The fear of stepping away from what's become comfortable, what's expected. It's the weight of expectation that's become ingrained in us all; it's what we all want to escape from but we all run back to. Gary got out and then came back; he knows the difference, but I still lose a little more of him each day."

I didn't quite know how to respond. "So you believe the people here are governed by fear?" I asked, not knowing if I was on the right track.

"I believe it's evil, not just fear. It comes from that stupid tree and that crazy cemetery. It's pure evil," Maggie said, her voice getting louder.

"You know, Shawn spoke of almost the same thing," I said.

"He knows—and he knows to get out of here. This place is evil; you know what it's like. It's like when you're in high school and there's a bully everyone is terrified of, but nobody will challenge them. Deep down, people know what he's doing is wrong. But they still strive to be his best friend or be part of the inner circle by doing things they know the bully will think is cool. I just don't get it." Maggie slammed her fist into the table.

I pondered what she was talking about, how throughout history, powerful, evil autocratic leaders would cast a spell over their people. It was these leaders' malignant narcissism and promises of success that drew some into their clutches—and fear of brutality that shackled others' will to resist. We weren't dealing with an evil emperor here—this was a spirit, a ghost of past, present, and future all wrapped into one. How could something not tangible create such mass community suffering? I guess the history teacher had started to take over in my thoughts again and rationalize the mysticism of this town.

I looked at Maggie and put my hand over the top of her fist on the table. "Well, I guess we're just going to have to punch the bully in the nose."

Maggie laughed and nodded her head yes.

"I hope you can see why I have to go back to the cemetery? Don't worry. I won't involve you in my midnight-caper plan," I said, smiling.

"You can't," Maggie said.

"What do you mean? I thought you understood that I had to confront what's out there!"

"No, you can't go without me. The Andersons have an elaborate security system. They put it in after the high school kids came and vandalized the statue of the Colonel and have been upgrading it every year since. You would think it was Fort Knox. Gary showed me ways around it. So, you see, I have to go with you," Maggie said, sounding hesitant.

"I see…so…are you up for this?"

"Yes…remember, I said I was all in. I'm sorry for being so hostile earlier," Maggie said, lowering her head.

"No worries, we all have our days." I smiled.

"Oh, I almost forgot to ask if you wanted to go with Gary and me to the Bear Creek Inn tomorrow night. They have a great band and half price drafts and…Shawn will be there," Maggie said, wiggling her eyebrows suggestively.

"Shawn! What about his ankle? I'm sure he doesn't want to see me anyway."

"Oh no, I think he's quite taken with you, and his ankle was just a sprain, so he's just a little gimpy," Maggie said, laughing.

"Well, like I said, I'm not interested, but I do like live music."

"Okay…sure…"

"So, can we go Friday night to the cemetery?" I asked.

"Yeah, that would be perfect. Friday's Gary's poker night, and he stays out really late. I can sneak his key card out before he leaves," Maggie said.

"Key card?" I questioned.

"Yep, they're high tech out there."

A loud pounding at the door broke up our conversation. I opened the door, and Emma Jean pushed by me, stomping into the room.

"Won't you come in, Emma Jean?" I announced, smiling.

Maggie giggled and quickly covered her mouth to hold it in. Emma Jean snapped her neck around and glared at me.

"What in heavens name are you doing here, Maggie May?" Emma Jean asked.

"I just stopped by to get my car," Maggie said.

"Is that all you're here for?" Emma Jean said in a slow southern, demanding tone, looking down her nose at Maggie.

I so wanted to say, *It's none of your business, you old bitty,* but I stayed calm.

"Well, of course, it is, Ms. Emma Jean. Why do you ask?" Maggie said.

"You've been up here for quite a long time just to be retrieving your car keys, and some people's company can be a bad influence," Emma Jean said in a snarky tone, looking squarely at me.

You bitch! I thought.

I was just about to say that, when Maggie stepped in and said, "To what do we owe the pleasure of your visit, Emma Jean?"

"I'm here to inquire about Mrs. O'Reilly's length of stay," Emma Jean said.

"I'm paid through the end of the month," I said, a tinge of anger in my voice.

"Yes…you…are…please remember that—and not a day longer," Emma Jean said as she headed toward the door, stopping and turning to make sure Maggie was following her.

"Maggie May, y'all need to come with me," Emma Jean demanded.

"Yes, of course, Aunt Emma Jean," Maggie said, turning her back to Emma Jean and rolling her eyes at me.

I put the car keys in Maggie's hand and said, "Thanks for stopping by, Emma Jean." Maggie giggled, and I slammed the door behind them, saying, "I hope you fall down the stairs and break your neck, you old bat!"

My patience was wearing thin with Emma Jean; I had thought of her as this colorful old busybody, basically the town gossip. Now, through different lenses, I saw her as hateful and mean. *Is the town culture rubbing off on me? God, I hope not.*

I decided to go shopping to get ready for my night on the town. This thought brought a smile to my face. Just thinking of shopping in Larksburg and a night on the town at a honky-tonk was hysterical. I was still a country girl at heart though, so this was right up my alley.

As I left my apartment, I glanced at the tree, which had consumed my every thought and action these past few weeks. For such a majestic pillar of mother earth, it held such a dark history; it seemed to be a crime against nature for it to have been used in such an evil manner. I hesitated, wondering if I should head out to the tree. Instead, I turned the corner and walked toward the clothing store.

The bell over the door rang as I entered the store, but I saw no one at first. Then a young store clerk popped from around the corner. It was such a relief to see a young person and not some old, grumpy biddy.

"May I help you?" she said with a smile.

I smiled back. "Yes, thank you. I'm looking for some cowboy boots, jeans, and maybe a nice blouse."

I hadn't worn cowboy boots since I was a teenager, and I couldn't wait to get a pair and have an excuse to wear them. The clerk directed me to the side wall where they had a display of women's boots. I saw the pair I wanted immediately, which was good because they only had four styles to choose from. I tried them on with some jeans and a powder-blue western shirt. Looking in the mirror, I was pleased, and I wondered if Shawn would like the outfit.

My face dropped. *What am I thinking?!* I couldn't discount the fact I was attracted to Shawn. My brain was in turmoil, thinking of betraying Joel for even a minute. However, I couldn't deny that my heart jumped a little when Maggie told me Shawn would be coming. I couldn't seem to reconcile my feelings with my loyalty to Joel. Every time I allowed myself to think of Shawn, I was racked with guilt.

The store clerk, reading my face, asked, "Is there something wrong? Would you like to try on something else?"

"No, no, this is just fine. I'll take it all, thank you," I said.

I changed back into my clothes and handed everything to the store clerk to ring up. Thanking the girl, I left the store and headed toward the market to get a boxed lunch.

The same husky butcher was behind the counter, but now, I had my order down, and the fun of harassing me was absent from his interaction. I grabbed my bag and glass of water and headed outside to my familiar table. I was shocked to see Josephine sitting outside because she hadn't been there when I entered the market.

A smile came to my face—I was so excited to see her.

"Hello, Josephine! How are you?"

Josephine kept her stoic persona and didn't respond immediately.

"Youse been busy, child, and please y'all need to call me Josie," she finally said.

Josephine had such a presence to her; she gave off a feeling of love through such strength. A love that made you just want to hug and hold her, coupled with a strength that made you want to be like her.

"What do you mean, Josie?" I asked.

"Youse met with the Colonel, didn't ya?" she said with what was the closest thing I had seen to an expression on her face.

"Well…yes…I did," I said.

Now knowing Josie could see all spiritual occurrences around her, I didn't question her abilities or knowledge.

"Will you help me?" I asked.

"Youse don't needs my help! God already put in you everything you needs. It be up to youse to use it or not," she said sharply.

"What has he put in me?" I said, shaking my head.

"Girl, youse needs to wake up, and look around. This place hasn't seen a rainbow across it for over a century. There are no colors of joy. Evil has seen to that," Josie said matter-of-factly. "Evil has a strangle hold on this here town — youse knows what happens when things can't breathe, don't cha?"

My mind quickly flashed back to my conversation with Shawn. How Shawn described this place as having all the beautiful colors sucked out of it. The emotional culture was basically soulless. I could feel my mind opening; it was as if a door had been pushed ajar and the wind of knowledge was blowing in my face. I could see—if only in my mind—how a bubble of fear and hate had formed like a dome over this town.

Looking at Josie, I stated, "I'll beat him! I'll beat the Colonel."

Josie laughed. "You never beat evil, but you can conquer fear. Fear gives evil power; without fear, evil is left dormant with no control."

I was at a loss for words, my mind racing, my emotions tangled. Before I could continue my discussion with Josie, her grandson appeared from inside the store.

"Okay, Grandma, time to get away from the crazy lady," he said.

Crazy lady! What a punk! I thought.

I grabbed my half-eaten sandwich and headed back to my apartment, still steaming from her grandson's comment. I stomped up my stairs and into my apartment; I sat down at my kitchen table and thought about what Josie had said, how fear feeds evil.

The history teacher in me took over again and examined evil autocrats throughout time: Herod the Great to Saddam Hussein. They ruled with fear, and fear built their empires, but they both met the deaths they deserved. The Colonel was not a ruler of a country, just a county, a town at best.

I realized it didn't matter the size of the evil siege; the only thing that mattered was the impact. Whether or not it's a leader of a county or the leader of a community, a president or a CEO, a bully's a bully. Those who surround them are willing participants, or those participants through victimization surrender to their fear. They fuel them through their emotions, not having the will to battle the attack. It's easier and safer to follow the pack, to join, or remain silent and survive. It's the passive people—or worse, those who seek power and prestige through obedience—that cause the wicked to grow. They create a furnace, fueled by the weakness of their souls, which becomes the coal that burns within evil. I started to get a sense of what lay ahead.

CHAPTER 12

SHAWN

I decided to spend the day at the library talking to Joseph before going out with Maggie May, Gary, and Shawn. I walked down the street taking in all the people. Their actions seemed almost robotic at times, the occasional wave to a friend or casual short conversation. It was all very plastic.

I stopped in Maggie's studio for a short conversation before heading to the library. Maggie was just finishing up a class with a bunch of ten- to twelve-year-old girls. I waited till they left before approaching her.

"Did I come at a bad time?" I asked.

"No, actually perfect timing. I don't have a class for another hour," Maggie said.

"Great! I just wanted to see what time I should be ready for tonight," I said.

"Is 6:30 okay? Oh, by the way, I heard you got some new duds for tonight!" Maggie said, winking and laughing.

"*I can't believe it!* Can I do anything without the whole town knowing about it?"

Maggie continued laughing and said, "Gary's cousin's niece is the clerk at the store."

"Oh, so a close relative..." I said sarcastically. This made Maggie laugh harder. "Seriously, Maggie, you haven't told anyone about us going to the cemetery tomorrow night, have you?" I was feeling a little nervous about this.

"Of course not. I do want to stay married you know!" Maggie exclaimed.

There was a long pause after Maggie's statement. "Well...except..."

"Oh, Maggie, you didn't!"

"I did tell Claire, only because she says you haven't been calling her enough, and we've become really good friends and—"

"Oh, thank god!" I said, relieved. "So what's the plan?"

"Well, the boys are going to friends' houses, and like I said, Gary will be at poker. The hired hands usually leave around nine to go to the bar and don't return until one or two in the morning. Clive and Hattie go to bed really early, so they shouldn't be a problem. I thought we would leave around 10:30 and get through the security and to the cemetery around 11:00," Maggie said, as though planning an operation for *Mission Impossible*.

"Sounds like you have it all worked out," I said. I could tell she needed to say something but was hesitating. "What...is there something wrong, Maggie?"

Maggie hung her head and said, "Well...are you scared? Because I'm terrified! I can't leave my children without a mother."

"Oh, Maggie, I'd never let anything bad happen to you or put you in danger."

"How do you know? How do you know nothing will happen?"

"Because I have faith." It came out of my mouth without me even thinking. Quick flashes of Jacinta, Joseph, and Josephine went through my mind.

I grabbed Maggie's hand, looked at her, and said again, "I have faith nothing bad will happen to either of us."

"Great! Would you mind sharing a little of that faith with me?" Maggie said, rolling her eyes. I smiled and told her I had to go, but I'd see her later that night.

As I walked toward the library, I felt great satisfaction from the end of our conversation, how the word and thought of faith came out effortlessly. I believed in not only myself, but all the powers that were guiding me through this journey. *This journey.* I thought back to the hospital and how Joel spoke of journeys. It brought a smile to my face instead of sadness to my heart.

"You're back," the librarian said with a sneer and the same judgmental coldness she'd always given me when I entered the library.

"Nice to see you too," I said as I almost skipped past her desk. I couldn't wait to see Joseph and talk to him about the Colonel.

I opened the door and spotted Joseph over by the window, watering some plants. "Joseph," I said, excitement in my voice.

He turned and greeted me with the warm smile he always had. "Well hello, Ms. Sara, and how are you doing today?"

"I'm great; thank you for asking," I said with a smile.

"To what do I owe the pleasure of your visit today?"

I stopped and thought for a moment, realizing I had never really told Joseph my story. He just seemed to know, or maybe I just felt like he knew without me telling him. The air became awkward and quiet.

"Well, out with it, girl!" Joseph demanded.

"Well, you know how I said, or alluded to, how I felt like...uhh..." I couldn't seem to find the words.

Joseph laughed, and I just stared, feeling embarrassed.

"Are you trying to tell me how you were called to be here? How you want to make a difference in this town, for the prisoners of the hanging tree?" Joseph said, opening his eyes wide and smiling.

"How did you know?" I said, surprised.

"Do you think you're the first?"

My shock at his comment brought my ego tumbling back to Earth. "Have there been many others?" I asked sheepishly.

"A few—not many—none like you," Joseph said, turning back to finish watering the plants.

I was scared to ask, but I said it anyway. "Is that a good thing or a bad thing?" This brought another round of laughter from him.

Joseph turned to look at me, paused, then said, "Come here, child."

I slowly walked over to him; he reached down and grabbed both of my hands and gazed into my eyes as if he were my loving grandfather. "I believe in you, and, yes, I think you are special, but what I think and feel is not of importance. This is on you, and your belief and faith in yourself. You have the ability to free all that have become captives of history."

I felt tears coming to my eyes. Joseph made me feel as though I were ten feet tall and could accomplish anything with his blessing. I felt so powerful yet humbled in his presence.

"Joseph, I feel the need to confront the Colonel, to stand up to him, to take him on, and conquer his evil," I said, clinching my fists and raising my voice.

"Now hold on; let me get this straight. You think going to battle with the Colonel is the way to take him down?" Joseph said, looking at me with a slight smile.

"Well...yes! Showing no fear to evil—is that not what all this has been about?"

Joseph chuckled again. "Child, you have all that talent, but you want to go toe-to-toe with the Colonel. Just what do you think that would accomplish?"

"I would show him that good wins out over evil," I said matter-of-factly.

"Hmmm, you're a history teacher, right?"

"Yes."

Joseph started pacing around the room, then stopped and looked at me. "In history, have there been leaders who created massive change without starting a physical conflict?"

I was feeling like the student and Joseph the teacher. "Yes, of course."

"Did these leaders throw bombs or start fistfights?" Joseph asked, in a somewhat condescending tone.

"Okay...okay...I get it. You're talking about Gandhi and Martin Luther King Jr., but they were not contending with an evil spirit that has encompassed a town!" I said.

"No, maybe just a nation..." Joseph winked, still smiling.

I pulled out a chair from the table and sat down, contemplating what he had just said. I took a deep breath, looked at him, and said, "It's not about the size or the power of the evil; it's about the righteousness of the actions taken to overcome the oppression. To believe in your heart you are guided by all that is right...you're guided by love. It's within the knowledge of decency...you will need no blood shed." I felt rejuvenated; the words came from my heart, without thought or trepidation.

Joseph smiled as if he were a proud papa. "Yes…you're finally listening to your heart and letting yourself be guided by love instead of anger, fear, and resentment. Remember this when you meet with the Colonel. He will gain no power from you—his control will diminish."

"What do you think I should do tomorrow?" I asked.

Joseph smiled, patted me on the shoulder, and said, "Follow your heart. God will be with you. Remember what you have discovered here today."

Before I could say anything else, a familiar voice came over the intercom, reminding everyone the library was closing early today for cleaning. I wanted to tell Joseph how much I appreciated him and how much he meant to me, but for some reason, the words didn't come. He squeezed my hand, and I lunged forward and gave him a big hug.

Joseph laughed and said, "You best be on your way."

I walked out of the library, my head spinning. I found a bench near the entrance and sat down. I felt different, like a weight had been lifted. My mind was swirling; I was a little disoriented. I wanted to just drive out to the cemetery or run to the hanging tree and talk to Josiah. I felt like I had knowledge that had been locked up inside for years, just aching to get out.

My phone rang, bringing me back to reality; it was Maggie May. I had almost forgotten about our night out. *How can I still go? It just doesn't seem right to go! Not now!*

I heard a voice deep down in my soul. It said, *Stay calm—your day will come.* It was Joel's voice; I just knew it.

"Hello," I said, answering the call.

"Wow, I was starting to think you weren't going to pick up," Maggie May said.

"Sorry, I was a little preoccupied. What's up?"

"I just wanted to check to see if it's okay if we eat at the bar tonight? They have really good food, and it's wings night. Gary loves buffalo wings," Maggie said with a chuckle.

I wanted to make up an excuse not to go. I just wanted to stay home and contemplate tomorrow.

"Sure, that'd be great," I said reluctantly.

"Everything okay?" Maggie asked.

"Yes…I'm just getting excited for tomorrow. By the way, I really want to get home kind of early, if it's okay with you?"

"I cannot believe you are excited for tomorrow—what are you, crazy? Don't worry about staying out late. We can't leave the boys home alone too long or they start fighting," Maggie said.

After we hung up, I walked to the apartment. I was still conflicted about tonight on so many levels. I felt uneasy about Shawn and my feelings of betrayal against Joel for even remotely thinking about another man. The thought of going out to have fun when I seemed so close to finishing what I was called to do in this town seemed wrong. I reconciled my thoughts with a realization—I hadn't done one thing for myself since Joel died. It was as if when Joel died, he took half of me with him. We were a whole torn apart, and without him, I was unsure who I was supposed to be. Even with all my newfound confidence, I still had a hole in my heart that just couldn't be filled.

I got dressed in my new duds, as Maggie would call them, and was starting to get a little excited about going out. As I peered in the mirror, I was proud of the way I looked— I felt like a real cowgirl in my new boots, which I loved. I couldn't wait to show it all off to Maggie.

A knock came at the door. I knew it was Maggie, so I quickly opened the door, anxious to show her my outfit. I was just about to say, *Hey, look at me*, when I realized it wasn't Maggie—there stood Shawn. I was shocked and a little taken aback by his presence. My heart jumped a bit. He had on a dark-blue long-sleeve button-down cowboy shirt, Wranglers with a belt that had a rodeo calf-roping buckle, and nicely polished cowboy boots. His hair had just the right amount of gray and was nicely groomed, hanging just above his collar; a Stetson was perched on top of his head.

"Uh...hello," I said awkwardly.

"Sorry for the surprise, but Maggie and Gary were having a little trouble with the boys, so they asked me if I could pick you up," Shawn said.

I was still a little shocked, and I thought that Maggie was setting me up. I stumbled with my words a bit but managed to answer, "No, it's...fine. It's...nice to see you again. How's your ankle?"

"It's fine. I was able to get my boot on this afternoon, a little bit of a tight fit but not too much pain, nothing a shot and a beer won't fix," Shawn said, smiling.

The way I was nervously stumbling around, I felt like I was back in high school. "Let me grab my purse, and we can go," I said.

"After you, ma'am," Shawn said as he politely ushered me out the door. As I walked by him to start down the stairs, I almost felt lightheaded in his presence.

As I turned the corner to go in front of the post office, I saw an enormous pickup truck. Thank God, it had step rails, or I would have never been able to get in. I could barely reach the door handle.

Once in the truck, I said, "Like a little truck with your pickup, do ya?"

It broke the ice a little. Shawn laughed and said, "This here is a small truck in Texas, ma'am."

"Oh, I forgot—everything is bigger in Texas," I said, a mischievous grin on my face.

"Yes, ma'am, you got that right." Shawn started the truck and gunned the engine for effect, glancing over and smiling at me.

When we pulled up to the Bear Creek Inn, I saw Gary and Maggie standing in the parking lot, waiting for us. Maggie quickly came to my side of the truck and waited for me to get down.

"Well, how was the ride?" Maggie said, giggling.

"What are you, thirteen? I told you I'm not interested, and I knew you set me up," I said, glaring at Maggie.

"No…no, the boys have been fighting like crazy lately; we actually had to hire a sitter to make sure they didn't kill one another. Basically, having a sitter almost killed them both," Maggie said, smiling with the satisfaction of embarrassing her boys.

We entered the club, Shawn walking by my side, being the perfect gentleman, pulling out my chair, asking me what I'd like to drink. I felt so safe with him, but yet I kept guarding my emotions, feeling there was something wrong. Every time I started to get lost in conversation with him, I'd pull back. I knew Shawn could feel it and was doing everything he could to help me feel comfortable. He even asked anything everything he could about my kids.

This was a trick Joel had taught my sons; he would tell them when in doubt, do everything you can to get your date to talk about herself; it will alleviate the pressure. Just the memory of the conversation Joel had with the boys about dating brought me a bit of peace.

After we finished our meal, the band started to play, and the guys ordered pitchers of beer. I hadn't had alcohol for a long time, so it didn't take long to feel a little buzzed. Shawn asked to dance, and I didn't hesitate to say yes; I loved to dance.

Shawn stood up, excited that I had agreed. I stopped for a moment and said, "What about your ankle?"

"The ankle is great now!" he said, which brought laughter from our table.

He took my hand, helping me to my feet; he then placed his opposite hand gently in the small of my back and guided me to the center of the dance floor. We moved around people until he felt like we were positioned correctly. He made me feel special, like we had to be in the middle so he could show me off.

Shawn was an excellent dancer. He spun me and twisted me to the beat of the music. I was having so much fun, laughing as if I had not a care in the world. It was the first time in a long time I had allowed myself to just have fun, and it felt so good. The music slowed, and Shawn clasped me in his arms and swayed to the music. I laid my head against his chest and melted into the moment. When the song was done, he gave me a little peck on the lips. I felt like I was on fire. I turned immediately and started walking to the table.

"Hey, wait, I'm sorry," he said.

I turned and said, "It's okay. I'm just tired, and I need to sit down."

When we returned to the table, Maggie was on her cell phone. She looked at me and said, "The babysitter just called. The boys got into a knock-down, drag-out fight over who would control the TV. She thinks that James broke Matt's nose. Anyway, I guess there's blood everywhere. So we have to go."

"Okay, let me get my things," I said. Shawn quickly broke in, saying he could take me home.

Before I could utter a word, Maggie replied for me. "Okay, that would be great. Why don't the two of you finish off this last pitcher," Maggie said, smiling at me. With that, Gary and Maggie were gone.

I sat down, feeling a little uncomfortable with everything that had transpired. Shawn looked at me and said sheepishly, "I hope it's okay with you? You know...that I take you home."

Shawn had been so nice and kind to me. I didn't want to hurt his feelings. "Shawn, this is all new to me. I haven't been on a date for a long time...I'm just not sure how I feel."

Before I could say any more, Shawn took my hand, looked into my eyes, and simply said, "It's all right."

There was a long silence before Shawn suggested we finish the pitcher and have another dance. After we finished, we made our way to the parking lot; I realized I'd had a little too much to drink, and my legs were a bit wobbly.

"Whoa," Shawn said, catching me as I stumbled while reaching up to grab the door handle of his truck.

"Sorry, I haven't been out drinking in a very long time." Shawn laughed as he boosted me up into the truck.

I rolled down the window and enjoyed the cool, fresh air as we drove home; it was helping me sober up a little. I told Shawn how nice the evening was, and he agreed. We laughed about him stepping in the hole at the ranch and how nasty Hattie and Emma Jean could be. He shared a couple funny stories about his sons, which made me feel even more secure in his presence. I could tell he was dedicated to his boys.

It wasn't long before we were at my door. I unlocked it and went in, but Shawn waited at the door. I turned and looked at him, not knowing what to say but feeling my heart beating out of my chest.

"Mind if I come in?"

I couldn't speak, so I just nodded my head yes.

He slowly walked toward me, stopping just inches from me, putting his hands to my shoulders and slowly moving them down to my waist. He gentle pulled me into his body. His smell was intoxicating; he placed his hand behind my head and pulled my lips to his. He moved from my lips to my earlobe and down to my neck. I melted into his arms as I felt his breath streaming along my face. I just wanted to wrap my body into his and get lost for eternity.

Shawn scooped me up and made his way to the bed, gently laying me down as if I were a priceless piece of crystal. He kissed me softly, and I returned his kiss, but then a feeling of profound sadness overcame me. I tried to fight it off, but I couldn't resist the power of the emotion. I started to cry...not just cry but sob uncontrollably. Shawn immediately stopped, and the mood changed very quickly.

Shawn didn't say a word; he just slowly slipped his arm around me and lay at my side, pulling me to his chest. I had never cried like this before in my life, not even when Joel died. I always felt like I had to be in control of my emotions to give off the illusion of strength. All of those previous inhibitions were gone, and I just let go; Shawn tenderly saw me through it.

I cried for what seemed like hours, Shawn holding me and comforting me through the night, never asking why. It was as if he knew everything I was feeling and needed no explanation. I slowly drifted off into a semi-state of sleep; I felt Shawn's arm leave my body and heard his boots on the floor as he exited without a word.

CHAPTER 13

REVELATION

I awoke to my cell phone ringing; I stumbled to the table where I had left it the night before. With my head swirling and my stomach churning, I answered the phone.

"Hello," I said in a groggy voice.

"What happened last night?" It was Maggie, and she seemed a little upset.

"What do you mean?" I asked, still trying to get my bearings as my head started to pound.

"With Shawn? He packed up his stuff in the middle of the night, texted Gary saying he had to get home, and he was sorry that he had to leave early," Maggie said, still sounding a little angry.

I sat down at the table and made a groaning noise. "Nothing happened last night. I had a little too much to drink and Shawn brought me home. He was a perfect gentleman, and we had a great conversation," I said, not wanting to divulge any of the personal details of my meltdown.

There was a pause on the other side of the phone and finally Maggie spoke with less hostility in her voice. "Well, why did he leave? Gary's blaming you, saying you must have upset him. He thinks you two got in a fight or something."

"No, there wasn't a fight. In fact, it was quite the opposite, and I really like Shawn. He's a good man, and I feel fortunate that I met him," I said, still not wanting to share what happened.

Maggie didn't want to let it go and probably knew there was more to the story. "It just doesn't make any sense why he would just pack up and leave in the middle of the night like that; it's not like him." She paused. "You know everyone is going to blame you! Clive will run you out of town," Maggie said indignantly.

I wasn't sure how to answer that, and I didn't want to share what was probably the most tender night I had ever spent with a man other than my husband.

I finally blurted out, "Well if everything goes well tonight, maybe they won't have to run me out—I can just leave."

That changed Maggie's tone and thought pattern very abruptly. "Tonight, I almost forgot about tonight!" she said.

"You're still in, right?" I asked, questioning Maggie's commitment.

"Yes, of course, but...I hadn't ever thought of you leaving. You've become such a lifeline for me. I haven't had a real friend since I moved here," Maggie said, sadness in her voice.

"Maggie, I have a life back in Colorado...my kids...my job. God sent me here to accomplish something...to help...to heal...to set this town free." I stopped and thought about what I had just said. It was what I had thought all along but was too afraid to verbalize aloud. My newfound confidence and sense of direction had allowed me the inner strength to voice my convictions. I awaited Maggie's response, fearing rejection.

"You think you were sent here to help us?"

"Yes…yes, I do."

There was a long pause before Maggie replied, "I do too…I've felt all along that you're here to remove the blanket of despair that's covered this community for far too long."

Maggie's confidence in me made my heart swell. I knew she was a gift to me on this journey, a gift of divine importance.

"Maggie, you know I couldn't have done any of this without you. No matter what happens, you'll always be my friend, and I'll keep you in my heart forever. Thank you for everything," I said, feeling tears coming.

I could tell Maggie was ecstatic to be included and to know our newly formed friendship would not end with my departure. She seemed to forget all about Shawn for the time being and was focused on tonight. We clarified the details and ended our conversation.

After I hung up, I noticed an envelope taped to the window of my door. *Oh great, they're evicting me!* I thought. I opened the door, grabbed the envelope, and brought it inside. It was a letter from Shawn.

In the letter, he told me not to worry about last night; he understood. He went on to say he was the same way after his wife died. Every time he tried to be with another woman, he fell apart. He assured me it would pass, as soon as I was ready to let my husband go and move on. He ended the letter by apologizing for his abrupt departure, saying he needed to leave to give me space, and when I was ready, he'd be waiting for me in Texas and gave his address.

I placed the letter in my purse for safekeeping, thinking about him. Women say there are no truly good men left in the world, but I would have to disagree. Shawn could have been angry or hurt by my behavior last night. Instead, he was a man of grace and compassion, not needing everything explained, having the confidence and faith in just being strong and calming. Shawn shared with me his own vulnerabilities and challenges, which made me feel closer to normal. I was sad knowing he had left, but I had to believe our paths would cross again someday.

My exhaustion from lack of sleep and consequences from drinking too much last night were still affecting me, so I decided to lie down and try to get some sleep, knowing I had a big night ahead. I drifted off quickly, and it didn't take long for my dreams to be engulfed by my ever-unfolding story.

I found myself in a white-satin cloud that reminded me of the one I was in when Joel lay in the hospital. I could see Joel; he smiled at me, told me that he loved me, and that he was so proud. I wanted to reach out and touch him, but I couldn't; his figure just wavered in the cloud. I felt no sadness; I was at peace and felt nothing but a deep sense of love. As quickly as Joel came, he vanished.

I was transported to the tree; Josiah was there, looking profoundly sad. I saw his wife and children in the distance. It looked as if they were trying to communicate with Josiah. Their faces were full of anguish because Josiah could neither see them nor hear their pleas.

Josiah disappeared from view, and a vision of Caleb and Ruth appeared; Caleb was on one side of the tree, and Ruth was on the other, both gazing out into the distance. A couple holding a baby seemed to be a few feet in front of Ruth. I knew it was Ruth's parents and her child. I wanted to run to them and physically push them together. However, I knew I was just a spectator and not a participant in this vision.

On the other side of the tree, a similar situation was playing out with Caleb. His mother, Mary, stood by a young man that I knew was Harold, just longing for acknowledgment from Caleb. I wanted to scream, *Go to them! They're right there!*

The pain of all involved was excruciatingly evident. Those who had passed on yearned to be united with their loved ones. The others were trapped by the evil of the tree and their own feelings of guilt and fear. I felt helpless and so inadequate.

Suddenly, lightning and a clap of thunder struck above the tree. It startled me, and I jumped at the sudden sound. When I recovered, I looked to my side, and there stood the Colonel. He looked at me with a snarling face and said, "They're not going anywhere."

I felt a surge of anger and yelled, "You don't own them, you evil piece of crap!"

The Colonel started to laugh wildly. The more he laughed, the angrier I got, and the larger the Colonel became. The wind was swirling and lightning was flashing around the tree. The Colonel now seemed to be over ten feet tall and was continuing to laugh and mock me. "You are no match for me! Why don't you just run home?" With a final clap of thunder, I awoke and sat straight up. I was drenched in sweat.

I jumped out of bed and ran to my window to look at the tree. It was a cloudy, overcast day, but there was a strange blackish-gray-tinged cloud hanging over the tree. I stared at the tree for several minutes before I decided to take a shower. Then I sat at my table with a cup of coffee in hand, thinking of everything that had happened in my dream. I loved seeing Joel; it always filled my heart.

Experiencing the possibilities that existed for Josiah, Ruth, and Caleb was heartbreaking. Seeing their loved ones through what seemed like a one-way mirror tore me apart. Is that what heaven is like? Everyone you ever loved standing and longing for your arrival, or is it just that way for the tortured souls stuck in between heaven and Earth?

The thought of their torture drove me even harder to find a way to set them free. I couldn't stand the thought of the Colonel holding them captive. The experience of being exposed to such an evil presence touched me deep down.

As you grow, your ideas of what evil is are somebody physically hurting someone else or causing irreparable damage. I have since surmised that those are evil acts; present here is pure evil—evil that controls actions and behaviors, which clouds, if not powers, people's lives. It's an evil that perpetuates continual pain and suffering.

I thought about my discussion with Joseph over my eagerness to conquer and Joseph's pulling of the reins to make me take a different route. Joseph's presence was so powerful, the feeling of love and forgiveness he emitted. When I first met him, I couldn't believe he could work in the Hanging Tree Museum. The mere thought of the atrocities that were committed at that tree made me ill.

I now realize Joseph's overwhelming power and spiritual dominance came from his ability to forgive. It was as if he opened his arms to the universe and said, "I forgive you, and I love you." The wider Joseph's arms spread the stronger his character became. How strong must you be to forgive centuries of hatred, racism, and brutality? Not just forgive but then want to be a keeper of history, to teach others of evil's existence and warn of its corruption.

I recalled the book that listed the victims of the tree and the ridiculous supposed crimes they committed. The pictures of the mobs at the lynchings—how could the onlookers just stand and watch. I surmised it was a way to show their dominance over people they feared.

As I sat sipping my coffee, I realized that everything in our personal makeup that's negative was tied to fear. Fear spawns anger, hatred, violence, racism, and bigotry; however, it became easier to label fear as evil. Evil left out the human aspect and responsibility for one's actions; it comes from childhood teachings: *"The devil made me do it."* Maybe there's a spiritual tie to communal behaviors, but how do you remove the power of fear?

While fear is the root of evil, love is the root of goodness. Love encompasses compassion, forgiveness, acceptance, kindness, and generosity. Yet it is easier to label love as goodness; the term is more palatable. Just as it is easier to label the universe as God, God loves and accepts all within the universe, his kingdom. Depending on your belief system, it all falls under goodness (love) equals God and evil (fear) equals Satan. It all seems fairly straightforward until you add the human element to the mix.

I believe this might be what Gandhi and Martin Luther King Jr. were able to see so clearly. If they could remove the power of fear from the grasp of the evil, the ability to control and manipulate would be stripped away. Evil could then remain dormant, and the power of love and the human spirit could prevail. Evil truly never disappears totally—it just lies in wait to be fed by those who provoke fear and discontent.

Joseph had taught me so much in the short time I had been with him—not just with his words but also his actions. I had such a hard time coming to grips with the thought of him being surrounded day in and day out with the memories of such a hateful history. He taught me that combatting hatred with more hatred only makes evil grow stronger. Capturing and surrounding hatred with love and forgiveness shows it for what it truly is—fear.

I was getting hungry, and with all of the thoughts of Joseph, I had almost forgotten about Josephine. I wanted to talk to her before tonight, so I left to get a sandwich from the store. As I approached the storefront, I didn't see Josephine in front at her normal perch. I was disappointed.

I went directly to the back of the store to order my usual sandwich, which brought about some eye rolling from the butcher. He placed my bag on the counter, took my money, placed the cup by the edge, and announced, "Here's a cup for your Perrier."

This of course brought laughter from the staff. I took my normal seat outside the grocery store to eat my sandwich. It wasn't long before Josephine's grandson wheeled her out so she could be in the sun. He stopped suddenly when he saw I was there; he seemed to be second-guessing whether he should leave her.

"Oh, I'm so glad you brought your grandmother out. I've wanted to talk to her," I said.

The boy looked at me and said, "You'd be crazy, lady." Then he left, shaking his head.

"Josie, I feel like I'm ready!" I said, leaning in to whisper in her ear.

"Child, may the grace of the almighty God and the protection of the archangel Michael be with you," Josephine said as she reached out and grasped my hand. Josephine had never moved before, so this caught me a bit off guard.

As she grasped my hand, a jolt went through my body unlike anything I had ever felt. I gazed at her face, and I could see her eyes for the first time through her black-tinted spectacles. They were a beautiful crystal blue, and her face seemed to be ebony porcelain; a feeling of power radiated from her body.

The screen door from the grocery store slammed, and the grandson and a very large man came out. "See, Daddy, I told you that white woman has been doing weird stuff with Grandma," the boy said.

"Lady, what in the world is you doing with my mother?" the large man said, glaring at me.

"I'm Sara O'Reilly, and you are?" I said putting out my hand to make his acquaintance.

"Name's Karl, not that it's any o' yer business, and youse still ain't answered my question!" Karl said angrily.

"I've just enjoyed visiting with Josephine; she's very kind," I said, smiling.

"Who's Josephine? My mother's name be Betsy, and she ain't spoken a word for almost three years, and she's nearly blind from a stroke she had, so, lady, I'm not sure who youse think you'd been talkin' to," Karl said in an angry, sarcastic tone.

"No, really, I've been talking to her. Josephine, explain to them," I said, trying to elicit a response from her.

Josephine stared straight ahead with no response.

"Lady, youse be crazy! She can't talk! You get out o' here, and youse leave my momma alone!" Karl said.

With that they wheeled Josephine back into the store, the grandson getting in one final blow, "Lady, you'd be nuts!"

I couldn't believe what had just happened. My head was spinning; I knew Josephine was real—I knew she was. *I have to talk to Joseph!* I thought. I took off in a near run toward the library. I ran up the steps and through the door. The librarian stood by her desk, telling me I couldn't come in because they were getting ready to close.

I pushed by her and said it would only take a minute. I just needed to talk to Joseph.

"Who's Joseph?" the librarian exclaimed, following me down the aisle of books.

We reached the back corner where the door to the Hanging Tree Museum was—it was gone.

"Okay, missy, I don't know what you're trying to pull here, but I told you we're closing, and there's no Joseph here, so you need to leave!"

"Where's the door? Where's Joseph?" I said, panicking.

I examined every part of the corner. Where there had been a door, a bookshelf now stood, labeled HANGING TREE HISTORY. I tried to get behind the large bookcase; it wouldn't budge.

"There has never been a door here...and no Joseph has ever worked here. What's wrong with you? Should I call Doc Smith or the police?" the librarian said, looking at me like I was mentally ill.

I slowly ran my hands along the books on the shelf, looking for answers.

"It was real. He was real," I said, feeling lost. "I need him; I need Josephine."

"Who's Josephine? I'm calling the police," the librarian said.

"No! Please don't. I'll leave," I said, walking away dejectedly.

"Damn crazy Yankees," the librarian mumbled as she walked back to her desk.

CHAPTER 14

GOOD VERSUS EVIL

I sat at my kitchen table contemplating my sanity. *Am I crazy? Did Joel's death push me over the edge? Could I be hallucinating people, places?* I grasped my head in my hands, wanting to scream.

I heard a voice from deep inside me—it was Jacinta: *You'd be a coward? Where's your faith, mon?*

Where's my faith? I thought.

While Joseph and Josephine may not be tangible, they were real, if only to me. I knew God brought them to me for a reason. They were brought to fulfill my journey. Fear and self-doubt left my mind and body.

My cell phone rang; it was Maggie.

"What in the hell have you been doing? The whole town's been talking about you! They say you've gone crazy! You raised a ruckus at the grocery, then went to the library, and were seen talking to a bookcase. Have you lost your mind?!" Maggie exclaimed.

"Well...I have not lost my mind," I said, hoping for no follow-up tirade from Maggie. I knew there was no possibility of that happening.

"Okay, well...would you like to explain? Because Gary doesn't want me within a mile of you!"

"Okay, I can tell you…but it might be hard for you to understand," I said, hesitation in my voice.

Maggie snapped back, "Gimme a try."

"You know the old woman at the grocery store? The one in the wheelchair?" I asked.

"Sure, everyone knows Betsy," Maggie said.

"Well…to me she wasn't Betsy; she was Josephine, a spiritual guide or angel who was sent here to help me," I said, waiting to gauge Maggie's response.

"What? That old woman can't talk!"

"Josephine, or Betsy as you know her, spoke to me, and in the library in the back corner there was a room called the Hanging Tree Museum, and a man named Joseph worked there and—"

"*Stop…stop!* I do not want to hear any more. Just stop! This is too far above my threshold of belief. If you tell me any more, I might back out tonight."

I could hear Maggie breathing hard on the other end of the phone, but she wasn't speaking, so I broke the silence. "You won't back out, will you?"

No answer from Maggie.

Then finally, she said, "No, I won't back out, but I do have some news that'll change our schedule a bit."

"What is it?"

"The poker game got canceled since Shawn left, so I'll have to wait until Gary falls asleep before I can leave."

"What time is that?"

"He likes to stay up late and watch movies, so it could be between one and two."

"What about the ranch hands coming home from the bar?" I asked.

"They're usually pretty drunk, so I don't think they'll be a problem."

"Okay, so will you call me when you're on your way here?" I asked.

"Yes, I will…and would you please do me a favor?" Maggie asked.

"Sure…anything."

"Please stay in your room and don't leave! The town is in such a stir—I don't need you adding any more," Maggie said, chuckling.

"I promise I won't leave until you get here," I said, echoing her laughter.

I decided to kill some time by making phone calls to the kids and Claire. It was so nice to hear the kids' voices and how happy they seemed. The boys were having a blast and didn't want to come home. They had only two weeks left of their trip, and they couldn't stop talking about all they'd seen. I could tell the love between the boys had grown exponentially, and they were definitely becoming young men. It was hard for me to say good-bye to them. I could feel their love flooding through the phone.

Ann was just as excited to talk as the boys; she was having a wonderful summer. Even though she had taken a short session of summer school, she had found some time to go camping and hiking. She told me of a beautiful hike she took in the San Juan Mountains, and she wanted to take me there upon my return. Ann asked how I was doing, and I told her I was doing great, enjoying the South, and having new adventures. This seemed to soothe Ann's inquisitive instincts and her worrisome nature.

I felt such an ache in my heart after the conversations with the kids. I missed them so much, but I was proud of the people they had become. I wished their father were here to enjoy them becoming young adults.

Claire was next on my list, and I knew she would probably not be happy with me since I had neglected calling her the last few days. I don't think the phone even rang once before Claire picked up.

"Well it's about time! What ever happen to 'Oh, Claire, don't worry; I'll call you every day'?" Claire said in a huffy, childish tone.

"I'm sorry…I know I'm a horrible friend." I chuckled a bit.

"Yes, you are…now spill it. I want to know everything," she said anxiously.

I began telling her everything. I told her about Shawn and I heard an, "Aw, how sweet." I went into great detail about Josephine and Joseph and my encounters with them and all that they had taught me. I explained how I was the only one who heard them or saw them, and now the whole town thought I was crazy. This brought a flurry of questions from Claire.

"So you're saying you went to a room in the back of a library that wasn't there and talked to a guy who never existed? Then you would go get a sandwich and have a conversation with a blind woman who can't talk? Hmmm, can't figure out why people think you're crazy…"

"Very funny, smartass. Do you want to hear the rest or not?" I said, chuckling again.

"Yes, of course, I do…you know I'm only giving you a hard time because I love you."

"I know, and I'm so lucky to have you. There's no one else in the world that I could tell this to that would believe me," I said with sincerity in my heart.

However, when I started to fill Claire in on my plan for tonight, she blew a gasket.

"Are you crazy! Did you not tell me some high school kids and a gravestone worker died after visiting that place! You're not going! If I have to drive to Larksburg tonight...you are *not* going!"

"Calm down; everything's going to be fine."

Claire wasn't buying any of it. "What are you going to do? How are you getting there? Does Maggie know about this?"

"Yes, Maggie knows. She's taking me. Maggie's the one getting me past the security system," I said calmly.

Unfortunately this set off another tirade.

"Security system! *Security system!* So now, not only do I have to worry about you getting killed by some evil spirit, I have to worry about you getting shot by the homeowner—or thrown in jail. Have you gone completely mad?" Claire screamed.

"Claire, please calm down. You have to have faith; this is what I was sent here to do. I know it in my heart and soul; Josephine and Joseph instilled in me a confidence...knowledge...a love and understanding I never possessed before. Or maybe I did possess it, but I never let it out. I feel like I've been given the grace of God, and he'll give me what I need tonight. God wouldn't have brought me this far to fail. I think I finally know my purpose—it was so simple and in front of me all these years."

"What? What's your purpose?" Claire asked in a pleading voice.

"To use my gifts to help."

"Yes, but to help whom?"

"Whomever God puts in my path."

"How are you supposed to help them?"

"I guess that'll be part of the challenge; I'm not expecting a road map for everything. I'm just expecting my faith in God and the universe to provide me with the grace to succeed," I said.

There was a long pause before Claire began to speak, "I hear it in your voice…you've changed…I always knew you were special and had special gifts. But now…now I hear almost a divine manner in your speech. I wish I were there with you." I could hear her crying.

"Claire, you're always with me. You've stood by me through it all, and never once has your friendship wavered. You are my true gift—I would never take that for granted," I said.

"Thank you, Sara. I'll still worry about you tonight, but I'll have faith you'll be all right, and if you don't call me when you're done, I'll never speak to you again."

With that, we both laughed. We said our good-byes, and I promised to call, and I told her not to worry.

I decided I would take some time to relax and listen to the radio. I really loved listening to the radio; the music always seemed to make me feel better. Just as I had turned it on and lay down on my bed to relax, there was a knock at my door. I looked at my clock; it was after 10:00, so I felt like it was too early for Maggie. I peeked through the curtain covering the glass. It was Arnold Anderson. I was kind of shocked to see him so late at night, but I opened the door.

"May I come in, Ms. O'Reilly?" Arnold said politely.

"Yes, of course," I said.

"I'm so sorry to disturb you at this late hour, but Emma Jean demanded that I talk to you," Arnold said.

"It's fine. I was just relaxing and listening to the radio," I said, noticing it was no longer playing.

Arnold walked over to the table where the radio was sitting and said, "Are you talking about this radio? The one on this table?"

"Well, yes…it's been great to have it. The music and talk radio has kept me entertained," I said, smiling.

"Ma'am, this here radio doesn't work. Hasn't worked for years; I don't even know why I keep it here. I guess for decoration," Arnold said, scratching his head.

"No, it works," I said confidently.

Arnold picked up the radio, and the cord dangled with just wires and no plug.

"I'm not sure how, with no electricity!" Arnold said, looking at me like I had two heads. "Ma'am, that's why I'm here. People 'round town, they've been talkin' and you…well you seem to be havin' some problems, ma'am. I'm usually one to keep out o' other folks' business, but Emma Jean, she just won't have it," Arnold said.

"Emma Jean won't have what?" I asked.

Arnold stammered some, and then he finally blurted out, "A crazy woman renting from us!"

"I see…so what does this mean?"

"Well, Emma Jean wanted you out tonight, but I said that ain't right, so we settled on next week," Arnold said, looking at the floor.

I felt sorry for Arnold and didn't want to make him any more uncomfortable than he already was, so I agreed, and he quickly left.

I sat back down at the table and grabbed the radio cord, examining the end and the bare wires. I rolled and twisted the cable with my fingers at eye level. I looked under the table, double-checking that there was not a plug somewhere. *How could this be?* I thought.

I thought of the music that played and the radio broadcast I'd heard. I reviewed the show from Reverend Al Sharpton talking about social injustices that have taken place now and in the past. The music was an eclectic mix of folk, country, rock, and gospel, every song or group of songs carrying with it a message of hope. It was those messages that had made me feel better.

My mind was starting to tie all the strands together; I could feel them being woven into a tapestry of belief. I realized the message was not just of Josiah's, Ruth's, and Caleb's salvation. It was bigger than just a few—it was for many. I remembered Joseph saying how we had to study our past mistakes to learn.

"We as a people must focus on what makes us the same, instead of our differences. Our differences make us unique and appealing but it is our commonalities that bind us. Those differences are our cloth but commonalties are our thread that connects us together. Makes us strong. If we could just see that, maybe we wouldn't fear each other. Maybe we could forgive a little easier and not hold past sins to eternity. We could learn where the path of hatred, fear, and division has taken us and that love is truth," Joseph had said.

I remembered the onlookers in the public-hanging pictures Joseph showed me. How angry I was that people would just stand there and not stop such an injustice. Certainly there had to be someone or some group of people who disagreed with the slaughtering of a race.

Maybe this was part of what I was to learn. Each of us every day make small and large decisions to pour gasoline on either the flame of good or the flame of evil. Do we stand by and watch? Do we join the chorus even through internal objections? God has given us all gifts; how we choose to use them can make all the difference. I choose to believe in the good of people. Even though through fear and social depravity, there are those who can easily be driven into hate, we must learn from our past mistakes and strive to do better.

Joseph has taught me well.

I wondered if this was what drove the Colonel; did something happen to him to make him hate so fiercely? Or was the evil innate from birth? This hate spawned generations following in his footsteps and clouded a whole town. I wondered if hate, for the Colonel, just became the easy way out of a bad situation—easier to hate and gain respect through fear and intimidation than to exhibit character and goodwill to his fellow man.

As my mind was reminiscing about the history of good and evil in the world, I laid my head down on the table and must have fallen asleep. A pounding at the door abruptly woke me; I jumped to my feet. I looked at my phone—five missed calls. *Oh no, it's 2:30. I missed Maggie's calls.* I ran to the door, opened it, and in rushed Maggie.

"Why didn't you answer your phone?" Maggie asked.

"I don't know. I fell asleep, but my phone was on the table," I said. I looked at my phone; for some reason it was on silent.

"I'm so sorry; is everything okay?" I asked.

"Yes, it just took Gary forever to go to sleep. He was pretty worked up about you and how the town thinks you're nuts."

"Yeah, Arnold told me I have to be out by next week," I said.

"What?!" Maggie exclaimed.

"Never mind, let's just get going. It'll be dawn soon and it's supposed to rain," I said.

We headed to her car. I noticed as we were leaving that Maggie was dressed as if she were part of a military operation: black pants, black long-sleeve shirt, and even black shoes.

As we got into the car, I said, "Geez, I feel underdressed."

Maggie rolled her eyes. "Very funny. I'm not taking any chances getting caught on camera and Clive and Hattie recognizing me," Maggie said.

"What do you mean? I thought you said you could turn it all off," I said.

"I can, but there's a camera that rotates around the security shed. If I mistime it, we could get caught on camera. I have to watch it until it rotates past the door, then run over and enter the shed, get on the computer, and shut down the system. Gary showed me how to flip a breaker to make it look like something tripped the power; with the rainstorm, no one will be suspicious. Lightning causes a shutdown all the time; they won't even check anything. They'll just come in and flip it back on and reset the system."

"Wow, I feel like I'm black ops or something," I said with a smile.

We pulled up to the iron gates that led into the Anderson estate. Maggie used the key card to open the gate.

"Won't the computer log who enters the property?" I asked.

"Normally, yes, but the cowboys disable the log on Fridays and Saturdays because they don't want Clive knowing what time they get home from the bar." We both laughed at the cowboys' ingenious plan.

Maggie entered through the gates and shut her headlights off; she knew the route well and had no problem maneuvering in the dark. She stopped the car, saying the security shed was just over the hill. Maggie grabbed a flashlight and told me she'd be right back. I wished her good luck as she grabbed a full-face ski mask and pulled it over her head. I couldn't help but laugh at how prepared she was.

"This is serious stuff here; I'd appreciate it if you wouldn't act like we're pulling a teenage prank!" Maggie said, sounding extremely serious.

"I know. I'm sorry, but since you're dressed in all black with a ski mask, you'd think we were robbing a bank, not visiting a cemetery," I said, trying not to laugh.

"Still not funny! Stay in the car," Maggie ordered as she closed the car door gently.

I could tell she was enjoying the cloak-and-dagger suspense and the danger of the mission. However, I knew there was more at stake for her than there was for me. Maggie wanted a sense of normalcy for her family; she wanted the Anderson hate, the curse, to be broken. Maggie saw her husband slowly turning into his father, and she didn't want that future for him or her sons.

I decided to roll down the window because it was getting hot in the car. I didn't notice the cow that had wandered up to my side of the vehicle. As soon as I rolled down the window, the cow mooed and scared me so bad I jumped clear over into the driver's seat. About that time Maggie returned, opened the door, and I nearly fell out of the car into the pasture.

"What are you doing?" Maggie asked.

"Nothing, just got spooked a little," I answered.

"If you're going to get scared by a little old cow, how are you going to handle the cemetery?"

"Don't worry; I'll be fine. How did everything go?"

"It was perfect; I felt like a spy," Maggie said proudly.

We started driving toward the cemetery when Maggie said, "Look," and pointed to the sky above it. It was glowing bright red, and the closer we got, the harder the wind blew.

Maggie looked at me and said, "Are you sure about this? I think they're expecting you."

I swallowed hard. "Yes, I'm sure."

When we arrived in front of the cemetery, the wind was swirling, branches and tumbleweeds flying through the air.

"No matter what you see or hear, do *not* leave the car. Lock the doors and stay inside," I told her.

"But…what about—"

"Do *not* get out of the car."

"Okay…okay…I won't get out of the car, but you better come back!"

"I will," I said, giving her a reassuring smile.

The wind was blowing so hard it was difficult to open the car door, and it was beginning to rain. I walked slowly to the iron gate; it was still slightly ajar from when Shawn and I were there. The cemetery seemed to be burning; I could feel the heat on my skin. I glanced over my shoulder back to the car and could see that it was under siege by spirits. I could hear her scream to me to go on. I hesitated for a moment and prayed for her protection—I knew I must continue.

I closed my eyes and asked God for guidance and to send the archangel Michael to protect me. Then I heard laughter coming from the granite statue of the Colonel. It was the most sinister laugh I'd ever heard. Then a flash, like a lightning strike, lit the sky.

A deep, bellowing voice said, "Scared, are you? Need help, do you?"

I saw a huge figure—it was the Colonel. He was glowing red hot and was almost as tall as the trees; flames shot from his hands. I knew I couldn't show or feel fear—that would only make him more powerful.

"I have my faith and belief in God, so I have all the weapons I need," I said, feeling the strength of my words deep inside myself. Again, a bellowing laugh erupted from the Colonel, and then another strike of lightning lit up the sky. My skin felt like it was going to melt from my body. I could feel fear enter. I had to fight it off. I thought of everything good in my life. I used my thoughts as fuel. I could feel myself start to grow, and a transparent shield formed in front of me.

I glanced back to check on Maggie. She was diving from one side of the car to the other; it looked like she was trying to hit the locks on the doors. The car windows rose and shut with velocity and force. Then suddenly the car was picked up and swirled around in the air, being tossed as if it had no weight. Something—spirits maybe—was rushing in and out of the car. A look of pure terror was on Maggie's face. Her screams now engulfed my thoughts. My size and shield diminished. I had to push it out of my mind. The Colonel was trying to control me.

"Oh, Maggie, forgive me," I muttered to myself.

"What do you think you can do here?" the Colonel said, drawing my attention away from Maggie.

"I want you to release the victims of the tree and remove your cloud of evil from this town," I demanded through the roar of the swirling wind.

With another bellow of laughter from the Colonel, the heat intensified. I looked at my hands, and it appeared as though my skin was melting off and falling to the ground. I knew he was trying to draw fear out of me.

I raised my hands to the heavens and said, "I have no fear of you, only love." I felt the heat lessening in my body. My size again grew and my shield returned. I felt a cool stream of peace flow through my body. Strength was building within me, and I could tell it worried the Colonel.

I continued to speak with authority, "With the power the universe has bestowed upon me, I forgive you and release from you all the evil power you have possessed."

The Colonel continued his laughter.

I filled my mind and soul with feelings of peace. I remembered what Joseph said about not combatting hate with hate. I was determined to take his power—not to feed it. I felt a cooling white cloud surrounding me, my protective shield strengthening with every word.

The Colonel tried shooting flames toward me, but they never hit their target. The cemetery was in a swirl of debris. Trees, headstones, coffins were caught up in the tornado with just the Colonel and I standing in the eye of the storm. I could hardly see nor hear the Colonel's shouts of superiority. I could feel myself growing stronger and more powerful. I had no fear. I felt total peace.

"Release your anger...your hatred—these souls are not yours for the taking. In doing so, you can be forgiven. Your reign of evil is over. You have fed on these souls long enough; set them free. Let love enter your presence, and you shall have your day with God."

The Colonel's size started to diminish; the fires that burned around me were extinguishing.

"You shall be forgiven," I said again and again. With each utterance of the phrase, the Colonel shrank in size.

The power of good was overwhelming his strength. I opened my arms wider, and the evil that surround him came to me in the form of a black cloud. I wrapped my arms around the cloud. It turned to dust and fell to the earth. For-giveness, while difficult, had removed the fuel that empowered his evil.

There in front of me was a small, shriveled-up old man. The once powerful, evil entity had been doused from existence.

The Colonel had surrendered, his head hanging down, no spirit of evil present.

"What does this mean for me? Will I ever be welcomed into the kingdom?" he asked.

I believed, at that moment, the Colonel might have al-ways longed for acceptance—not only in his human life but also in his spiritual existence. What propelled him to go that path we might never know. The lure of power or the product of abuse or a combination of both seems to breed and feed evil that exists in all. Whatever it was, it was powerful enough to follow him into death and gave a soldier to the wicked lurking army. Fortunately his time of wreaking havoc on this community had come to a close.

I walked closer to him to get a sense of his sincerity and for final proof of his submission. A sense of relief seemed to radiate from his tortured soul.

The Colonel again asked what the future would hold for him.

"Only God can grant you absolution. I have forgiven you in order to release the captives of the tree and break the spell on the town. Forgiveness grants freedom to the victims, not the wrongdoer. What happens to your soul is up to God. But until that time, you must stay within this iron fortress and never expel your evil on anyone again," I said.

Stripped of his supernatural power and his place in the unearthly, the Colonel nodded, turned, and disappeared. I slowly walked back to the car, physically and mentally drained.

I opened the car door to find a very frantic and disheveled Maggie. Her hair was standing almost straight up, as if she'd stuck her finger in a light socket. Debris was scattered throughout the car.

"Whoa…what happened here?" I asked.

In a growling voice, Maggie said, "I hope you had a good time! Because I went through hell out here!"

I smiled and said, "Well, I don't think you'll have to worry about that happening again."

On the drive back to town, Maggie gave me the blow-by-blow description of the nightmare that had happened to her outside the cemetery. I let her talk because I could tell she was fairly traumatized. It seemed like no time at all, and we were pulling up in front of the post office. Maggie stopped abruptly and said, "Oh no, not again."

As we gazed out to the tree, it was aglow, fire red just like the cemetery. Maggie started to squirm. "I can't go through that again!"

I wasn't sure what to make of this; had the Colonel tricked me? I told Maggie to go home because it was almost dawn. She didn't want to leave me but knew she'd better get home before Gary and the kids woke up. I watched as she drove off.

I walked out to the tree. I could see Josiah pacing and Caleb and Ruth sitting quietly, looking down at the ground. I was shocked to see them still there; I thought after the Colonel had relinquished his evil, they would have passed on. "Why are you still here?" I asked.

Josiah stopped, glared at me, and said, "Yeah, we felt the Colonel's chains being broken, but you think we'll be welcomed on the other side?!"

I realized that while it was hatred and evil that put them here and chained them to this tree, it was guilt and fear that now kept them bound.

"What...you think God is up there waiting for you with a club? You are his children! None of what happened to you was your fault; you have done no wrong," I said, pleading with them to understand.

Ruth stood and said, "I got pregnant by a white boy; my parents were devastated!"

"Yes, and I've seen your parents and your child; they're waiting for you, Ruth," I said, feeling the prick of tears in the back of my eyes.

"You've seen my child?" Ruth asked in disbelief.

"Yes...they wait for you; go to them, Ruth," I pleaded.

Ruth seemed to embrace the thought of seeing her parents and her child. In the distance, a voice called out, "Ruth...honey..."

Ruth looked at me, shock obvious on her face.

"Go to them," I said. Ruth ran into the white-satin cloud that had now surrounded the tree, and then she was gone.

Caleb was next; he stood and approached me and said, "Do you think I, too, could be accepted?"

"Of course, Caleb. God made you; you, too, have done nothing wrong; your loved ones wait for you—go to them," I said, a steady stream of tears now flowing down my face.

Caleb started to walk into the cloud but stopped, paused, and turned around, saying, "Thank you." I waved, and then he, too, was gone.

Josiah stood with his back to me and said, "It's not that easy for me, you know."

"Why is that, Josiah?"

"I've done bad stuff…I betrayed my own people…got people killed…didn't protect my wife and kids. No God will forgive that! Neither will my wife and kids."

"Josiah, you are loved, and the forgiveness you seek needs to come from yourself. Your wife and kids wait for you; you must let go. The shackles of the Colonel only provided comfort in your misery. Shackles of evil you did not earn; God sees all and forgives. Just let go, Josiah," I said softly.

Josiah turned to me slowly, his face frozen in anguish, and said, "I'm not sure I can."

Then, through the clouds, a vision of Josiah's family appeared, and a small voice pleaded, "Please, Daddy, come home…come home to us."

A smile split Josiah's face. "That's my boy! And look, my wife and little girl. I'm comin', baby…Daddy's comin'!" Josiah ran to the arms of his family and disappeared in the cloud.

I dropped to my knees in exhaustion, then I heard a familiar voice—it was Joel.

"You've done great, babe. You just have one more soul to let go."

I arose and looked at him, so thankful for his presence, and said, "What do you mean? Who are you talking about?"

"Me," he said.

"What? What! No! I need you! You can't go! Please, Joel!" I said, crying uncontrollably.

"Sara, I stayed to help you see your destiny and fulfill your purpose, but it's time for you to let go of me, so we both can move on," Joel said, consoling me.

I looked over his shoulder, and in the distance I saw Jose, Jacinta, Joseph, and Josephine standing in the meadow; I stopped crying for a moment and stared.

Joel looked at them and back at me and said, "They were your guiding angels; a piece of them exists within you, Sara. Angels exist everywhere, disguised as humans for those with sight."

"Then why can't you stay and be my angel?" I shouted.

"It doesn't work that way. I'll always be with you in your mind and heart, but I need to move on, Sara, and so do you. You can do a lot of good for so many. The light shines bright in you, and helping people is your calling." Joel gazed into my eyes and stroked my arm.

I didn't want Joel to be held to this Earth because of my selfishness, but my heart couldn't bear to let him go.

Joel brushed my hair out of my face and wiped away my tears and said, "You'll be fine, and the kids will be fine, but it's time for me to go." He kissed me and gave me one last hug, then walked into the meadow. Jose, Jacinta, Joseph, and Josephine also turned and faded into the distance.

In the meadow was also a long line of people who I knew had to be the other victims of the hanging tree; one by one, they turned and disappeared into the cloud. The tree had let loose all the souls it had possessed. I turned my attention back to where Joel had walked into the distance. He turned, smiled, waved, and was gone. My heart fell, but I knew he was in a good place; while his existence died, his love would live on. His love would beat in my heart and the heart of his children forever. Joel was gone from this Earth, and I had to move past his absence, but I would never move on from the love we shared together.

The sun was rising as I turned to walk away from the tree. A smile came to my face as I witnessed the most beautiful rainbow I had ever seen, which shined brightly over the town, the dome of evil lifted. The soul had returned to Larksburg, and its people had been released from darkness into the light of a new day.

A new beginning born from love and forgiveness. It was time to go home.

Made in the USA
Monee, IL
28 February 2020